BIG MAMMA & CELESTE

By AUDREY LEWIS

Published By
Milligan Books

Cover Design by
Tim Alexander, ASAP

Published and Distributed by:

Milligan Books,

an imprint of Professional Business Consultants

1425 W. Manchester, Suite B,

Los Angeles, California 90047

(323) 750-3592

Second Printing, January 2000, Printco Graphics

10 9 8 7 6 5 4 3 2

ISBN 1-881524-50-7

DEDICATION

Not only do I dedicate this book lovingly to my two sons, Frankie and Aaron Lewis, who have continuously supported my dreams and ambitions, but I give a very special thanks and most gracious acknowledgement to their father, Frank Lewis, who encouraged me to write, and then assisted me in doing so.

ACKNOWLEDGEMENTS

Thanks to Tim Alexander and Joe Schmeeckle at ASAP for their timely and creative talents.

A special thanks to the Jordan, King and Lewis families. You are my life.

BIG MAMMA
&
CELESTE

EMMA'S PRAYER

Search me, O God, and know my heart,

Try me and know my thoughts,

And see if there be any wicked way in me,

And lead me in the way everlasting.

Psalm 139: 23-24

Chapter 1

She sat on the old wooden steps outside her back woods Louisiana home crying as she listened to her mother and her mother's boyfriend fight. The beautiful little girl was devastated. She was only ten years old and the only two people she had ever loved were about to send her away and she didn't know why. She asked herself over and over again what she might have done wrong, but nothing came to mind. Why would

Marcus want to send her away? She tried her best to please him. Why did her mother agree to it? She always did what her mother told her to do. What could she have done to merit such heartless punishment? She just couldn't figure it out. Twice she attempted to go inside the house and discuss it with them, and both times she was shoved back out the door by Marcus, yelling, "I told you to shut that damned door and stay outside 'til I call you!"

Yes, he drank a lot, but she didn't care about that. She loved him. He had been with her mother most of her life. He was the only father she knew. Yes, he smacked her around once in a while, but maybe she deserved it. Maybe it was because all the little boys in the area seemed to like her. She was a fun-loving little tomboy who could beat any boy at his game, including baseball. So the boys would always let her join in. But that couldn't be so bad, she thought.

Her mother was seldom home, and when she was she consumed about as much alcohol as Marcus did, and wouldn't hesitate to use the milk money to buy cigarettes. But Emma Celestine Bouvier, who sometimes only got one meal a day, loved them both with all her heart, and did not want to be sent away to an orphanage.

Roscoe was a nine-year-old mangy mutt that had been given to Emma by her neighbor when she was three. The fuzzy and twisted gray hair on the dog's back was so sparse it looked like somebody had given him a perm and left it on too long. His whiskers hung over his mouth like an old man's mustache. But, Emma loved him in spite of his looks. Her little heart was always open to each of God's precious creatures whether it crawled, ran, jumped, flew or swam. She loved everything and everybody. Her mother use to tell her that one day she was going to be a Veterinarian. But Marcus would always find a way to stop Emma's dreams. Probably, because he had no dreams of his own. He used to tell Emma that all she was good for was to be a whore because she was always looking at boys. Always trying to get some man's attention. Emma was only 10 years old! Most of what Marcus accused her of she didn't even understand. What was a whore? All she knew was that it had something to do with men and women, and something dirty. One day she asked her teacher and she got smacked with the teacher's paddle, and all the kids laughed. You just didn't talk about such things in 1938.

Roscoe slowly approached Emma as she cried. He didn't like seeing his best friend unhappy, so he tried to make it better by licking the tears from her cheeks. It worked. She hugged him for comfort. Being of Creole blood, Emma had inherited a healthy head of long black hair. One of her soggy wet pigtails hung over Roscoe's face blocking his view as she held on to him, but he didn't mind. He just sat there quietly with both paws up on her lap, leaning against her, wanting to protect and soothe his sad little owner whose two piece cotton playsuit was saturated with wet salty tears.

Marcus was a big man who seemed mad at the world. He was so self-centered that he was convinced that every man in town wanted his woman, and he was positive that every job interview was set up just to put him down. And even though he had an incredible ability to retain anything he read, or solve any problems dealing with math, he somehow had convinced himself that he would never amount to much. His beautiful white teeth and gorgeous dark, flawless skin, combined with his broad muscular shoulders, made him a stunning male, but that didn't help. Marcus just couldn't cope with the real world, so he drank, wanting desperately to make the pain of hopelessness go away.

Emma's mother was a French-Creole beauty. Everybody thought she would become a famous star of some kind, but Marcus put a stop to all that talk. He was a jealous man whose constant criticism and displays of anger beat her down so badly she gave up all hopes and dreams of anything worthwhile. He did a good job convincing her that she was no good, so she spent many years trying to make herself worthy of this angry man she so deeply worshipped. And now he was about to do the same to this most precious and innocent child. Emma was about to get a full dose of her play-father's so-called love.

Marcus burst out the front door. Roscoe jumped quickly off the porch. He didn't want anything to do with this man. "Get in here, girl!" Emma moved fast, but not fast enough. Marcus pushed her inside the kitchen where her mother sat quietly with painfully red eyes. She said nothing, nor did she reach out to console her frightened daughter.

"We're sending you away so that you can get your act together." Marcus said.

Emma was upset. "But what did I do, Daddy?" She started to cry, but this didn't affect Marcus. As a matter-of-fact, he seemed to get some enjoyment from her tears. "You're no good - like your mother, and I want you outta here! I'm tired of feedin' you and takin' care of you. It costs money, and I ain't got enough to spend on a worthless little piece of shit like you!"

Emma was so hurt she didn't know what to do. She cried and cried. Her mother cried too, but strange as it may seem, made no genuine attempt to defend her helpless daughter. Emma's mother just sat and let it happen as if she was some sort of pathetic robot waiting for her master to tell her when to speak. At one point she stared at Emma for a moment and then turned to Marcus. Emma was sure that her mother was finally about to come to her defense, but it didn't happen. Her mother just got up and walked out of the room, staring at Marcus only to make sure that he didn't hit her again as she squeezed by him.

The next day Emma was gone, picked up in a big black car and sent away to spend the next eight years of her life in one orphanage after another - never to see Roscoe again.

Chapter 2

Esther Rose was a bitch. Growing up during the Depression made her stingy, self-centered and mean. She was determined never in her lifetime to be caught without money or a man. Everything else was secondary. She would re-heat leftovers until they tasted like paper. One chicken would last for days no matter how many mouths were fed, and then she would boil the bones for soup. If somebody gave her a gift she wouldn't use it. Once she received a lace nightgown for her birthday and she put it in a drawer until it rotted. She said she was keeping it for a special occasion. For her wedding somebody gave her a beautiful set of lamps that stayed in the attic so long, the fringe fell off the shades and the lamps turned a moldy green.

In the thirties & forties Esther Rose took in orphan children. She had a garden out back and chickens out front, and she generally made their clothes out of used tablecloths or old curtains. She tried to convince people that she was doing this for the good of the children, but she wasn't. She was lazy and greedy, and used the children as an excuse to get money from anybody willing to give it to her.

Esther Rose didn't like to clean the house so she made the children do it while she spent most of her time eavesdropping on the telephone party line, or in her bathroom pulling facial hairs from her chin. She looked like she had more man in her than the average man.

Esther Rose was sure she had everything under control - that is, until she met her newest homeless child, Emma Bouvier; a fourteen year old pregnant Creole beauty who would kick anybody's ass if they so much as looked at her the wrong way. But Esther Rose was determined to get along with this one because she knew there could be extra money in it for her. She had decided that she could make a good little chunk of change on this new baby, depending on how it looked when it came out. If it turned out to be as light-skinned as the mother, she could sell it to some rich white family that wouldn't be able to tell the difference until it was too late. But young Emma had other plans for her baby. She knew what it was like to be literally thrown to the wolves, and she wasn't about to let that happen to her precious new offspring. She knew that if somebody had given her just one ounce of the love and attention that she so desperately needed, everything would have worked out better for her. Emma had made up her mind that this baby would always be a part of her life, and they would live happily ever after. And not even this smiling old White woman standing in the doorway wearing too much make-up, and smelling like lilac perfume, was going to change that.

* * * * *

Emma screamed in agonizing pain as the local midwife probed inside her uterus, trying to turn the baby around so that it would not be a breech birth. And even though the young mother-to-be was wrenching in pain, she never regretted being in this situation because she knew that the future joy of her life was about to be born. But the midwife was worried. "This doesn't look good. I think we need to call a doctor."

Esther Rose stood close by, making sure that this new addition to her pocketbook came out right. "We're not calling anybody! That costs money."

Esther Rose was so adamant about having this baby born secretly that she pushed the woman aside and was about to try and pull the baby out herself. The woman could not believe Esther Rose's behavior.

"What are you doing, Miss Rose?" She yelled as she fought off this crazy ole lady. Esther Rose was desperate. "Get out of my way, you Black bitch! This baby is going to be birthed right here in this house. This one is mine!"

The midwife did everything she could to keep Esther Rose away from the little mother-to-be who was obviously in excruciating pain.

Suddenly Emma let out a loud, earsplitting scream as baby 'Celeste' popped out of her mother's womb, ripping the walls of Emma's vagina wide open causing blood to shoot everywhere. The two women stopped momentarily to stare at the bloody sight lying motionless on the edge of the kitchen table. They couldn't believe what they had just seen. It was as if the impetuous little newborn suddenly decided that it was coming out regardless of the difficulties.

The midwife was sure that the baby was dead so she approached the limp little creature carefully as she prepared to cut the umbilical cord.

Emma was exhausted, but not too tired to ask about her little bundle of hope. "Is it okay? Is it a boy or a girl? Is it all right? Talk to me!"

Nobody answered her. They just started trying to revive the bloody bundle. Emma couldn't stand the suspense. She pushed herself up on her elbows trying to see what was going on. "What's wrong? Is my baby okay? Give it to me!"

But they couldn't give it to her because it was so tangled up in the umbilical cord it appeared to have choked to death. For one second the two women looked at it in horror, and then the midwife began untangling the bloody mass. The moment she got the cord from around the infant's neck and cut and pinched it off, Esther Rose snatched the baby by its ankles. She then hung it upside down and whacked it so hard it flew up in the air almost hitting the overhanging light, at which time the naked little infant blurted out a resounding cry for 'life.' The exhausted midwife could only respond by saying, "It's a girl, missy."

Esther Rose practically threw the little tot back at the midwife and walked out of the room. What a way to enter this world.

Emma really enjoyed her first two weeks breast feeding her baby. For a while it looked as if she wouldn't be able to do this because of her age and her tiny breasts, but Emma came through like a champ. She was the perfect mother, and Esther Rose exhibited model behavior as a caretaker and parent. "Why don't you let me do your hair? I'll put some color in it to make it look better."

At first Emma was delighted by the offer, but after living with so many dishonest people she had learned to be suspicious of kindness. "Thanks, but no. The dye might do somethin' to my milk."

"It won't do anything to your milk, silly. All it will do is give you back your youthful look. You are so young and pretty. Don't throw that away just because you had a baby. You'll never get a man that way."

Emma thought that sounded pretty good. "Maybe Esther Rose's intentions weren't bad after all," she thought. "Maybe it's time to stop being so paranoid about people." So she consented.

"Good! I'll go into town in the morning. I know just the

right color for you."

Emma couldn't believe that Esther Rose was being so nice. Maybe things will be all right here, she thought. Maybe staying here won't be like the other places. She started to smile as she looked down at her precious little fair-skinned, green-eyed darling baby girl.

Esther Rose and Emma had fun trying to figure out how best to bleach out the rich dark color of Emma's hair. After working their way through that, and then looking through magazine after magazine, picking out the right hairstyle, it was done. Emma was a blonde bombshell. When she looked in the mirror she was surprised at what she saw. Esther Rose had done an amazingly good job. Gone were the long heavy black braids inherited from her mixed Black and French ancestry. Emma's hair was so beautifully set that it looked as if she had just come from an expensive downtown beauty parlor. Esther Rose stood behind Emma, watching as she stared at herself in the mirror.

"If I didn't know better, I would think I was a White girl with all this yellow hair." Emma said as she ran her fingers gently through the long blonde strands. "It's kinda pretty." Emma flung her hair back and forth to make it bounce.

"I told you you'd like it. And you're right, you could pass for White if you had a mind to."

On Sunday afternoon Emma and baby Celeste set out for their usual afternoon walk. The old used stroller that Emma had gotten from the church sure came in handy. The big awkward wheels were not easy to maneuver over the rocks and ditches in the dirt road, but Emma managed. The two of them enjoyed their daily strolls. The smell of the fresh country air and the sound of birds singing in the trees were so peaceful. Emma never dreamed that she could be so happy.

Coming down the road was an unusually large black car. Emma noticed it quickly because she had had a lot of experience with big black cars, but she had never seen one as shiny and beautiful as this. She stopped in her tracks so that she could see who was inside the car as it passed her by. She stood still and waited to spot some big mean-looking man sitting behind the wheel with some ugly old woman on the passenger's side, leaving town after picking up some poor unfortunate child to take to another God-forsaken orphanage.

Emma stood erect as the car approached. Expecting the worst, she was pleasantly surprised when she saw a good-looking young White couple inside, with nobody in the back seat. They both looked at her and her beautiful little baby and smiled. She returned the greeting and went on her way as the soft warm wind blew softly through her blonde coiffure. What a perfect day, she thought.

Life finally seemed good for Emma. That is, until that same couple she had seen on the road in the big black car showed up at Esther Rose's house the following Sunday.

Looking out the window, Emma recognized the car immediately because she remembered the big emblem on the hood and the words Rolls Royce on the back. What a funny name for an automobile, she had thought.

The couple got out of the car and entered the house with

Esther Rose holding on to them like they were long-time buddies. Emma rushed to the top of the stairs inside the house
where she could see Esther Rose escorting the handsome pair
into the living room. Emma thought it was strange that they
seemed to know each other so well without her ever having
seen them at the house before. And what was even more
strange was when Esther Rose left the living room and returned
with Baby Celeste in her arms, at which time she handed the
infant to the woman who held on to her with so much love and
admiration that it frightened Emma. None of this made any
sense. She just didn't know what to think as she raced down
the stairs determined to interrupt this strange setting.

Esther Rose was surprised to see Emma standing in the
doorway. "Oh, I thought you were taking a nap. Emma, this is
Mr. & Mrs. Duboineau." Emma thought the woman seemed nice
and genuine enough at first. However, this nice stranger was
holding on to Emma's last possible link to any happiness, and
that didn't sit well with her at all. Emma quickly snatched the
baby from the woman and left the room without saying a word
to anybody. She could hear Esther Rose apologizing for her
behavior as she rushed up the stairs to her room. Esther Rose
ran after her, demanding that she come back downstairs with
the baby, but Emma kept going. She made it to her room in just
enough time to slam the door and lock Esther Rose out. Esther
Rose was furious at her. "You little whore, I will get you for
this!"

Emma sat on her bed and held her tiny bundle of hope
tightly, and sang aloud in order to drown out the sound of
Esther Rose beating in the bedroom door, demanding that she

open it and come back downstairs.

Night fell and Emma was still holding Baby Celeste securely in her arms.

Emma didn't speak to Esther Rose for weeks. She didn't ask who the people were nor did she try to make amends for her behavior, and for some strange reason Esther Rose didn't demand an apology nor did she offer an explanation. They just lived together in silence. The only voice heard throughout the house was the not-so-frequent cries of Baby Celeste demanding her share of attention. And she didn't have to make demands too often because her loving, now fifteen-year-old, mother was seldom out of her sight.

Emma's hair was black again. She'd figured out the purpose of the White girl look, and wanted no part of it. She made sure to cut off every strand of that bleached blonde lie. Now only the black roots of her hair were showing. The inch-long beautiful waves lay just right against her head, and looked pretty good even though it was an odd style for women in those days. But this style was easy for Emma to take care of, especially with the baby and all. She liked it.

* * * * *

Just when Emma was finally getting the hang of being a mother, the Social Service lady was waiting downstairs to take away the only thing that mattered to her, her new born infant. Esther Rose had finally managed to get her way. Emma was being sent to a reform school, and her baby was about to be adopted by an 'unknown' rich young couple. Yeah, right. Emma knew exactly who the rich young couple was, and she knew that Esther Rose was behind it all, but she couldn't do anything about it. She was just a kid. Tears flowed as Emma packed up the baby's things. "Why does everythin' happen to me?" she wept.

When Emma reached for Baby Celeste's stuffed animals they reminded her of her old best friend, Roscoe. So much emotion built up inside her that she had to stop packing and sit sullenly on the side of the bed. Through the open bedroom door she could almost see Roscoe racing up the stairs to greet her with one of his big sloppy licks. Oh, if only things could go back to the way they were when she was little, she thought. She also began to think about her mother. She smiled as she looked over at Baby Celeste who was sleeping quietly, only to be interrupted by a loud yell from Esther Rose. "Emma, these people are down here waiting for you!"

Esther Rose knew that Emma wouldn't answer her so she suggested that the Warden and the Social Service lady go upstairs and get her and the baby.

The moment Emma heard footsteps at the bottom of the stairs she was overcome by fear. The reality that they were indeed coming to get her and her baby finally set in. So, despite the sound of thunder outside, Emma jumped up from the bed, and without hesitation, snatched up the remaining diapers and threw them in the cloth bag and flung it over her shoulder and then rushed over to Baby Celeste. Without a second thought, she grabbed the sleeping angel, climbed out of the window on to the attached lattice and carefully, but hastily, escaped down the side of the house while clutching her baby under one arm.

Emma raced across the dark back yard and out the back gate. She didn't worry about the fact that the old wooden means of access banged shut behind her. Her attention was completely focused on escaping this awful nightmare. She knew that she only had a few minutes before Esther Rose and her posse would be out there looking for her. Holding on dearly to her precious little baby, Emma ran across the lonely road to anxiously await the first vehicle willing to give her and her baby a ride to the nearest Greyhound bus depot.

Emma stood on the side of the dark road waiting to hitch a ride. She had been through so much in her young lifetime that the fear of running away was not an issue. Despite the low clouds, and smell of rain approaching from the east, it never occurred to her that a storm was brewing. She was confident that there was nothing out there that could be any worse than what she had already experienced. But, it wasn't over yet.

While clutching Baby Celeste tightly in her arms, Emma felt something wet on her cheek. She quickly wiped it away, but just as soon as it was gone, she felt another wet spot. It had started to rain. Emma was about to cover Baby Celeste's face with the blanket when she noticed something strange. The baby was completely silent. At first, Celeste thought how great it was that her little darling had remained so calm and quiet throughout this ordeal. She rubbed her forefinger gently across the baby's face with affection. Her heart was filled with so much love for Baby Celeste. But when Emma's hand touched the infant's face, the baby's head fell to one side in an unusual manner. Celeste tried to get a better look at her through the dim moonlight. But because of the dark low clouds, visibility

17

was difficult. So, despite the light rain, Emma pulled the blanket completely off the baby's face to get a better look.

"Celeste?" Emma said as she shook the baby. "Are you alright, Honey?" But, the baby didn't move. So Emma shook her again, and yelled, "Celeste? Baby? What's the matter with you?"

Something was wrong with Baby Celeste. The child wasn't breathing. Emma panicked. She didn't know what to do. A million things went through her head. "This can't be happening," she thought, as the rain began to come down harder.

"Oh, God, please don't let this happen to me right now." Emma begged aloud. "Please don't take my baby!"

A light appeared in the distance. A truck was coming. Emma got excited. Still holding dearly on to Baby Celeste, she started to wave it down, but the truck rushed on by. Emma couldn't believe this was happening. For a moment she thought about running back to the house, but she knew the consequences of that. If the baby was dead, she would be held responsible, and she would be put away forever, and if it lived it would still be taken away from her, and she would still be locked up for running away.

Suddenly her sense of survival took over. Emma sat down on the damp ground and began to apply artificial respiration, which she had learned in reform school. However, nobody had taught her how to administer this to an infant, but she tried anyway. Emma carefully tilted the baby's head back and began to breathe into its mouth. One, two, three... One, two, three... The downpour of rain made it even more difficult for Emma's wet hands to massage Baby Celeste's little chest, but Emma worked at it best she could. And finally, she succeeded. The baby coughed, sucked in air, and then began to cry. Emma had held her so tight while escaping from the house that she had almost smothered Baby Celeste. "Oh, thank you, God!" Emma cried aloud. "Thank you." She cried again. "I promise I will take care of her good! Just don't let anythin' happen to her again, please." And almost as if God was responding, another light approached. Only this time the car stopped to pick her up - seconds before a tremendous downpour of rain. Emma was relieved as she held and patted her infant child in an attempt to stop her from crying. As she rocked and fed the baby, the car whisked her off to the bus station to call her mother and tell her that she was coming home to Louisiana with her new born baby girl.

Chapter 3

The bus stopped one half mile from the house, and Emma's mother, Rachel, was there pacing back and forth, anxiously awaiting her long-lost daughter and her brand new grandchild. Marcus had left her, so the timing could not have been better for the two women. Unfortunately, it didn't last very long. Emma had experienced more in her fifteen years of life than the average woman of forty, so it was almost impossible for her to adjust to the strict rules her mother placed on her, especially after Emma hooked up with her childhood friend, Lena.

Lena was a beautiful and troubled teenager. Her dark brown velvet skin was flawless. She loved the attention of men, was addicted to cigarettes, and spent most of her time 'partying'. Emma was so starved for affection that it didn't take long for her to fall right in with Lena's crowd. The two beautiful young girls had the men of this backwoods county wrapped around their fingers. They were given anything they asked for, and they asked for a lot.

Emma let her hair grow back, and as soon as she turned eighteen years old, one of her men friends bought her a nice car and kept Baby Celeste in the best of clothes. Emma tried to share her small fortune with her mother but she wouldn't accept any of it. She told Emma that she didn't like where the money came from. This didn't bother Emma. She had become a very cold and calculating young lady who took whatever was offered and demanded things that weren't offered. Her belief was, "Take it before somebody else gets it."

Emma needed desperately to punish somebody for something but she didn't know what it was or who it should be. She just knew that she was downright mad at the world, and she was determined that somebody would pay for her pain. So everybody paid. Everybody, that is, except Lena and her baby. Those were the two special people in her life. Her mother, the built-in baby-sitter, came in fourth, after the money.

Once Emma's mother found out that Baby Celeste was a result of Emma being brutally raped by one of her foster parents, she made an extra effort to be more patient with her troubled daughter. Plus, the guilt she carried all those years for allowing Marcus to abuse Emma was a lot to bear. She was sure that this was the reason for Emma's uncontrollable anger and low value on herself. So when Emma would act up, she would threaten to put her out, but she never did. Plus, she was afraid that Emma would take the baby with her. She had grown so attached to her new grand daughter that she couldn't bear the thought of living without her.

Electrical storms in the South can be deadly because of so many trees. Emma's mother was a witness to that. In the South you learn very early not to stand under a tree in an electrical storm or run through the woods during that time because tall trees serve as conductors and you stand a very good chance of getting struck by lightning. This was what had happened to Rachel when she was a child. So one of her rules was that nobody goes out during a storm. But Emma had someplace to go, and Lena was waiting outside in the car. So the best way to get out of the house was to start an argument. And Emma was good at that. She knew that if she made her mother angry enough, nothing would be said about her leaving the baby again. She knew that her mother would be glad that she was gone.

Emma never sat down and actually planned arguments. Usually she would say, "I just need to get out of this house so I can breathe."

But when the mean side of her would come out she'd carry the fights too far. For some unknown reason Emma enjoyed putting her mother down. It seemed to give her a sensational thrill. "Now I know why you were so glad to have me come home. You were scared! Like I can stop lightnin' from strikin'. Ever since I can remember you been scared of somethin'. If it wasn't the lightnin' it was Marcus. You were probably scared of my daddy too. I wouldn't be surprised if he didn't die of a heart attack. You probably ran him away and just lied to me so that I wouldn't go lookin' for him. He's probably out there somewhere right now lookin' for me and I don't even know it. He was probably a good man until you got hold of him with your constant whinin' and fearin'. I don't know why I came back here. You get on my nerves so bad! How in the world did you get to be so damned pitiful?"

Frustrated because her mother would not give her enough ammunition for a good battle, Emma dug deeper. She had a tendency to get so caught up in the motion of fighting, she would forget that the sake of the argument was only to get out of the house. Emma may not have been Marcus's real daughter, but she sure acted like him. She got a sick pleasure out of seeing her mother cry. "Look at you! You're not good for nothin'! I can't wait to get the hell outta here!"

Lena got tired of waiting for Emma so she got out of the car in the rain and came up on the porch and watched as Emma and her mother fought. She had seen them go at it before, but this particular night seemed more intense. So intense that Lena even got caught up in the moment and made the big mistake of interfering. "Why do you even bother with that 'heifer.' She don't know what she's talkin' about. Let's get outta here. We got things to do, girl." The moment Lena called Emma's mother out of her name, the fight took a full about-turn.

Emma spun around to Lena, with eyes blazing. "What did

you call her?"

Lena didn't hesitate to say it again. "She's a heifer! A cow! She's always moanin' and stuff. I don't see how you can stand it. She's pathetic."

At that moment Emma was on Lena like white-on-rice. Because Emma was taller and bigger, it didn't take much for her to pin Lena against the wall, ready to beat the living daylights out of her. "Don't you ever in your life call my mother a name again, you understand?"

Lena was surprised at Emma's reaction. She thought, at first, Emma was playin', but when she looked into Emma's eyes she knew that this was not a joke. The anger was so intense that Emma was shaking and perspiring all over. Her fist was raised and ready to come down on Lena with full force, but luckily Rachel stepped in to stop her. She approached Emma slowly and directly. By now Emma was choking Lena so tight around the neck that she could hardly breathe.

Emma's mother's voice was soft and gentle as she stroked Emma's back. "Emma Celestine Bouvier, don't hit that girl. She ain't done nothin' to deserve your hittin' on her." It was as if Rachel was seeing Marcus all over again. "She didn't mean to call me that name, did you, child?" Lena was anxious to respond. "No - ma'am, I - didn't and - I'm sorry." Her words were barely audible.

Lena's best friend had turned into somebody she didn't recognize. Never in her life would she have imagined the possibility of her ace boon-coon beating her within an inch of her life, but it had almost happened. "I'm sorry, girl. I didn't mean it."

Emma stood over Lena and stared her in the eye as if she never heard a word Lena said. Being from the streets Lena knew not to say any more. She just looked at Emma and waited. It took a moment, but Emma finally lowered her hands at which time her mother breathed a sigh of relief. And even though Lena was about to die of fear, she played it off real cool-like. "You ready to go now?"

This seemed to ease the tension as Emma replied, "Yeah."

Both girls straightened out their clothes, grabbed their purses and were off to run the streets, not to be seen by Emma's mother or Little Celeste for two to three days.

The storm was exceptionally fierce that night. Rachel sat upstairs in the dark and counted after each flash of light. One, one thousand, two, two thousand, three, three thousand, and so on. When she made it to ten she rested easy because that meant that the lightning was at least ten miles away. But when it struck within the count of one or two, all of her fears returned. She held Little Celeste in her arms and sat in the corner in the dark and waited for the storm to subside.

A few weeks later one of Emma's boyfriends bought a lightning rod for the house and explained the purpose of it. That helped a bit, but by that time Rachel had already made her decision to move to Atlanta, Georgia to be with her family. That is, if she could get Emma's permission to take Celeste with her. She knew that if she could just get Celeste away from this hell hole things would be all right. She knew that she could raise this one better than she had her own. This time she wouldn't let anybody else come between them. This time she would make up for all her mistakes of the past.

Emma sat on the back porch holding Baby Celeste and singing to her like she used to when they were with Esther Rose. Rachel watched through the curtain, waiting for the right moment to tell her that she was leaving. But her two girls seemed so peaceful that she didn't have the heart to disturb the moment. So she waited.

The next day Rachel was down in the basement throwing things away. She knew she had to tell Emma sooner or later, and later just kept feeling better and better. But the time had definitely arrived because when Emma walked up to the house all she could see was old clothes and junk flying out of the basement window.

Inside the cellar Emma quietly watched her mother go through old boxes and dusty trunks. "What are you doing?"

Well, there was no time like the present, her mother thought to herself. "I'm gettin' rid of all this junk because I'm movin'."

"You're what?"

"I'm gettin' the hell outta here, and I'm takin' Celeste with me." There, she finally said it, and boy did she feel better.

Emma had never heard her mother curse before so she was caught off guard. "What are you talkin' about?"

Rachel stopped as she was going through a trunk of old clothes. There, in the bottom of the big suitcase, was a black and white picture of a handsome Negro man. Rachel rubbed her hand softly over the old wooden frame. "I'm movin' back to Atlanta."

"You ain't been to Atlanta in twenty years," Emma remarked

sarcastically. She couldn't believe what Rachel had just said.

"I know. It's time I went home."

Rachel remained composed as she continued to hold on to the old photograph of her dead husband. It was almost as if that picture was now the key to her newly found strength.

Emma had never seen her mother like this before. For a moment, the thought of being left here alone sent a slight sense of fear through her body. She didn't know how to respond to this new person, but she was determined to try. And as usual Emma couldn't do it without insults and degradation. "Have you lost your mind? You don't have enough guts to move across the street! How do you think you can manage to get to Atlanta?"

As hard as she tried, Emma could not make her mother cry.

"I'll be leaving on Thursday, and I'm taking Celeste with me." Rachel said with conviction.

"Like hell, you are!" Emma screamed. "You, Bitch! How dare you try to take away my little girl!"

Emma went after her mother with the same intensity as she had with Lena, but this time there was nobody there to calm her down. She charged at her mother with full force, but in return, got the surprise of her life. Rachel suddenly reached back with all her strength and landed a smack so hard across Emma's head, that Emma stumbled backwards and fell over the opened boxes. Emma was shocked. Her mother watched her fall and never blinked an eye. "You will never in your life raise your hand or your voice to me again, do you understand?"

Emma couldn't speak. She just sat there and stared at this

menacing 'stranger' hovering over her, breathing heavily, ready to strike again.

"I loved your father with all my heart, and when he died my whole world stopped." Emma's mother held back her tears and continued. "I was young and had a baby on the way, and didn't know how I would make it. My parents were poor, and I was even poorer. When a man came along and offered to take me away and help me, I accepted. I had no idea Marcus would turn out to be so mean, and I would end up in this God-forsaken place."

Emma sat still on the floor and waited for her mother to finish.

"You get this through your head. I never cried because I was weak. I cried because it hurt me to my heart to see you actin' like - Marcus. And yes, I'm scared of lightnin'. I ain't gonna lie about that. And I challenge anybody who's been struck by it to tell me they ain't scared either. Maybe I need to get God back in my life so that I can overcome it, but if it started lightnin' right this minute I'd be scared again, and that's a fact! But that don't make me no fool. I'd be a fool if I stayed around here and watched you ruin your life."

Rachel was so filled with emotion she could hardly breathe. But, she didn't cry. She just kept talking as if she had been waiting a long time to get all this out of her system.

"Emma, I am truly sorry for lettin' Marcus treat you that way. God only knows how sorry I am, but I was so scared of him, I didn't know what to do. He beat me so many times I couldn't count. He put me down so much I couldn't feel nothin'. So I am sorry, daughter. I am truly sorry for everything you been through."

Rachel reached out for Emma, expecting her to respond with open arms, but she got a surprise too. Emma just sat and stared at her in cold silence. This love-hate relationship was over. There was nothing left in Emma's heart but hatred. And if Rachel took the baby away, the likelihood of Emma's heart ever being repaired was slim to none, and Emma knew it.

Chapter 4

As the years went by Emma grew even more ravishing. But behind that beauty was a mean and calculating Creole woman. She knew how to use every inch of her sensuality to get whatever she wanted from whomever she wanted. Nobody got close to Emma Celestine Bouvier. If there had been one ounce of compassion left in this female it was destroyed when she lost her loving baby girl, to Rachel.

Celeste, now sixteen years old, was doing well back in Atlanta Georgia with her grandmother. She was definitely growing up to be one of the most beautiful young ladies in the city, but her naiveté sometimes made her appear to be a bit backward, not to mention the way she wore her hair. Celeste had long, thick black hair like her mother's, and could have worn many attractive hairstyles, but Rachel intentionally insisted that she wear two ugly braids that stuck out over the sides of her ears. Rachel told Celeste that the braids were good for the hair, but it was simply one more way of keeping Celeste ill favored to the opposite sex.

Rachel had kept such tight reins on Celeste that it was nearly impossible for the shy young girl to know how to relate to other young people. She seldom played with the other children because she always had to come home right after school. She only knew about life through books. And Rachel made sure that the books she read did not include sex. Rachel was determined not to make the same mistakes she had made with Emma. The only problem with that was that she almost created a misfit of a different sort. If it had not been for Celeste's ninth grade school teacher, Miss Henderson, who seemed to understand her better than anyone, Celeste would not have even known that it was natural to have started her menstrual period. Miss Henderson gave her several pamphlets to read about general health. When Celeste took the pamphlets home to show to Rachel, Rachel snatched them from her and tore them into little pieces and forbade her to ever talk about such things again.

Rachel felt so threatened when Celeste came into her womanhood that she began working even harder to keep Celeste away from outside influences. Rachel was determined that neither the young boys of Atlanta nor their dirty old fathers were ever going to get their hands on her little girl. She used every trick in the book to keep Celeste in the house, including guilt, which seemed to work the best. Rachel's problems ranged from bad headaches to the infamous electrical storms.

Miss Henderson was a tall and handsome African American woman. Her square jaw, short-cropped graying hair and chestnut brown complexion were striking, to say the least. Her makeup always looked natural. Her wine-colored lipstick seemed to match perfectly with her lightly applied rouge. She was just the opposite of Rachel, who insisted that makeup was the work of the devil.

Miss Henderson was a strong and loving teacher whose only concern was for her students. Her deep melodious voice demanded attention, and Celeste gave in willingly.

One day Celeste tried to leave school early because an electrical storm had been predicted and she knew that her grandmother would be frightened. Miss Henderson did not give her permission to leave. She explained to Celeste that she had to allow her grandmother to deal with her own problems. She helped Celeste understand that there were times when she must concentrate on what was best for her. Celeste embraced the advice, thus becoming a stronger, but still somewhat unpolished young girl.

Regardless of Celeste's eccentricities, she was a fine looking, well-read teenager, and could certainly amount to something if given the opportunity. But suddenly all possibilities of success went straight out the window when Rachel received a letter from Emma requesting that her daughter be returned home. Rachel was horrified at the thought of Celeste going anywhere near that house of iniquities. So she responded...

Dear Emma,

I can tell by your letter that you are doing good. I'm glad to know that you miss your daughter. I know it's been a long time since you've seen her. I feel bad when I think about how I took her from you, but it was for her own good.

I hope you will forgive me some day for all the things I let happen to you. I was young and weak-hearted and I am truly sorry. But even though I know you hate me and I would like for that to change I cannot send Celeste to you right now. She is a good girl and will be graduating from high school next year. Maybe when she's twenty-one she can come to see you.

Your mother,

Rachel

It wasn't one week after Rachel sent the letter back to Emma that Emma showed up at Rachel's doorstep ready to hurt anybody who would try to stop her from taking her daughter home.

As Emma stood on the porch smoking her cigarette and ringing the doorbell, she could see the curtain inside the window move gently aside. Emma knew somebody was in there. She placed one hand on her hip and pointed her cigarette at the small opening in the curtain with her other hand. "Open this door, Rachel. I know you're in there."

Quietly the clean, tightly drawn white-laced curtain stopped moving, but nobody opened the door. This made Emma even angrier. She stomped her foot so hard her heel almost went through the porch floor. "Rachel, if you don't open this door I'm gonna break it down!"

Rachel hadn't told Celeste about Emma's letter. She had hoped that this whole issue would go away, but obviously it had not. Emma arrived well prepared to take her namesake home.

Celeste didn't remember her mother. So, this buxom and overly made up woman, dressed in red and black sexy, low-cut clothes with spike high heels and long black hair, standing on the other side of that front door was a complete stranger to her. Needless to say, Celeste didn't know what to do. If this had been close to Halloween, Celeste might have considered opening the door. But it wasn't Halloween, and her grandmother hadn't told her that they were expecting guests; especially a guest that looked like this. So, Celeste just stood there peaking through the curtain at this noxious cloud of smoke circling this crazed woman who was shifting from one high heel to the other, and constantly adjusting her straps on her slinky silk dress. She was obviously angry. Celeste continued watching as this woman banged on the door and called out her grandmother's name over and over again.

"I'm not goin' away, Rachel!" Emma shouted.

Finally, Celeste got up enough nerve to respond. "Who are you and what do you want? My grandmother's not here!" Celeste yelled.

When Emma heard Celeste's voice it stunned her for a

moment. She knew that it must have been her daughter on the other side of the door, but she wasn't ready to deal with how grown up Celeste sounded. Emma hadn't seen Celeste since she was a baby. And now that she was about to become face to face with her, there was a moment of tremendous regret for all the years of not attempting to see her only child. But it didn't take more than a few seconds for Emma to get back to her old angry self. She was not only angry because she couldn't see who was hiding behind that curtain. She was angry because she couldn't control her feelings of guilt and neglect. She was angry because she didn't know what to say to this now obviously young adult. And even more so, she was angry because Emma just didn't know how to be any other way. So, what should she do now? What else? Be her own bitching self and curse somebody out!

"I don't give a damned where your grandmother is! If you don't open this door, I'm gonna start breakin' out every one of these tacky-ass stained glass windows. I'm your mother, and I came to take you home, so open this damned door!"

Celeste couldn't believe what she was hearing. Was this really her mother? Looking and sounding like this?

"Good Lord, this must be some kind of joke," Celeste thought to herself. But before she could make a decision one way or another the window in the front door was blasted apart by the force behind Emma's over-sized purse. Colored glass shattered everywhere. Celeste was shocked and frightened, but had her own courage. When Emma reached through the broken window and unlocked the deadbolt latch and then burst through the door, Celeste just stood there and stared into the eyes of this large buxom woman whom she had never seen before.

"Who are you and what do you want?" she asked. "I told you my grandmother's not here!"

For a brief moment Emma just stared back at Celeste. She was not prepared for what she saw. Celeste was a rare beauty. Emma had never seen anybody so clean and pretty in all her life. For a brief moment, Emma felt a little uncomfortable. For that same moment she was sorry that she had intruded the way that she did. But, as usual, Emma quickly got over it. "You must be Celeste," Emma huffed.

"Yes, I am." Celeste responded with conviction.

"Well, I'm your mother, and I came to take you home."

Celeste's grandmother had not prepared her for this. Rachel had always tried to make Celeste think that her mother was someone special. But Celeste found nothing special about this woman.

"I ain't goin' nowhere with you, lady. I don't even know you!" Celeste shouted. The thought of this crazy woman saying that she was her mother was absurd. One part of Celeste wanted to run in the corner and cry and beg this tacky person to go away, but another side of her was curious, so she stood her ground.

"Who are you?" Celeste asked without hesitation. Emma was not accustomed to anybody having the courage to get that close to her without her permission. Once again she was speechless. But as usual, it didn't take long for her to recover.

"I am your mother." Emma replied as she moved in closer

to Celeste, who, to Emma's surprise, didn't budge an inch.

"Like hell you are." Celeste snarled. She was not about to give in to this situation. Miss Henderson had told her that she had rights, and she wasn't about to let anybody violate them again, especially a stranger that looked like this.

Emma was so impressed by the spunk of this young girl that she couldn't do anything but back down herself. She could see a lot of herself in Celeste. She slowly began to remember all the love she had had for her baby girl. So Emma decided to stop fighting. But she wasn't going to go down nicely. It would be against her nature.

"Why are you wearin' those ugly-ass braids in your hair?" Emma asked sarcastically.

"They're my braids and I like 'em." Celeste responded. She had had to defend herself so many times at school and this was no different.

"Well, you need to get rid of 'em," Emma shot back.

"Well, you need to get rid of some of that makeup!"

"That's none of your business."

"Neither is my hair your business."

"Your hair is my business because you are my daughter."

"You ain't proved it by me." Celeste seemed to be winning again. "I ain't never seen you before in my life."

"You're a smart mouth little shit, ain't you?" Emma was sick of this game. Besides, she was obviously losing, and she didn't like it one bit. She knew that if this continued she would probably do something that she might regret. Something like smacking Celeste in her mouth if she didn't shut up.

Finally Rachel showed up. And the moment she saw her favorite stained glass window shattered into a million pieces, she suspected that Emma had something to do with it.

Rachel had not forgotten about Emma's uncontrollable temper, so she approached the matter cautiously as she entered the foyer.

"Emma, it's good to see you." Rachel glanced over at Celeste and was relieved to see that Celeste was holding her own.

"Celeste, how did the window get broken?" Rachel asked. But before Celeste could answer, Emma interrupted. "I did it. Your granddaughter wouldn't let me in, so I opened it myself."

Even though Celeste was a little shaken, she still insisted on getting some answers to what this woman had been telling her.

"Grandma, who is this woman?" Celeste asked.

Rachel tucked her head shamefully. "She's your mother."

Celeste just stood there staring at Emma. This was definitely not what she had imagined her mother to look like. Celeste saw similarities in the hair, but then her eyes followed Emma's oversized and partially exposed breasts all the way down to her 3-inch high heels, and she immediately decided that this had to be a joke. But even though she had never seen anything like this woman before, she was not judging Emma. She was judging Emma's actions.

"What are you lookin' at?" Emma asked sarcastically. Once again this child was making her feel uncomfortable.

So many thoughts ran through her head. "How in the world did she bring something so clean and fresh into this world?" she thought. "How does someone stay so fresh and shiny?" Emma just couldn't get enough of Celeste's beauty. A small part of her wanted to touch Celeste's soft velvet skin to see if it was real. For the first time she remembered how wonderful it use to be to caress her little baby girl. For the first time in a long while she thought about how she would hold baby Celeste and sing to her. For a brief moment all she wanted to do was to hug this girl and tell her how much she missed her. But the major portion of Emma's clouded mind told her to just take care of business and get on with her plans. So she did just that. "I came to take you home."

"This is my home." Celeste responded.

Rachel was nervous because she realized that she might have to come between the two women she loved most. Rachel remembered the incident with Lena and Emma, and knew that she did not want that to happen in this case because Celeste would not be as forgiving as Lena was. "Emma, would you like to sit down? Rachel asked calmly. Emma ignored her. She just stood there looking at Celeste, who stared back.

"Emma, did you get my letter?" Rachel asked.

"I got it, but it don't matter. Celeste is comin' home with me." Emma said as she continued to stare down Celeste. She made no attempt to look at her mother, whom she hadn't seen in over fifteen years.

Rachel didn't know what to do. Obviously a lot older now, Rachel had no intentions of hitting Emma the way she did before leaving Louisiana. Besides, Emma is a lot bigger than she used to be, and definitely a lot meaner, and probably would kill Rachel if Rachel attempted to touch her. "Emma, please don't take my child away from me." Rachel begged. "She's a good girl, Emma. She don't need to be in that house with you."

"Your child? She ain't your child. She's mine and she's comin' home with me. Now!" Emma's anger was so intense that she didn't realize that her cigarette had burned all the way down to her fingers. She never even felt the heat.

"Put the cigarette down, Emma. You're gonna burn yourself." Rachel said.

Still staring at Celeste, Emma flicked the butt on the floor and didn't attempt to put it out. Luckily, it had almost burned to the end.

Rachel was so filled with despair that her chest felt like a ton of bricks had fallen on it. Her legs were heavy, and her arms were numb. She couldn't do anything but stand there and watch. Celeste, on the other hand, stood strong without a whimper. Even though in her heart she was frightened, she refused to let this woman know it. One might say that this was definitely one of her mother's traits.

"Go and get your shit!" Emma snapped at Celeste. But Celeste didn't move. Rachel stood motionless with a slight tear running down her cheek. "Emma, please..." Rachel begged.

"Shut up, woman!" Emma yelled as she snapped around toward Rachel. In that second Celeste was sure that Emma was about to hurt her grandmother, and she wasn't going to let that happen.

Suddenly, Celeste grabbed a nearby lamp and charged at Emma. "Don't you touch my grandma!" Celeste screamed as she raced toward Emma, who was too quick for her. Emma had

41

fought so many fights in her lifetime that she could smell an attack before it happened. Emma reached for the lamp and snatched it out of Celeste's hand, and was about to hit her with it when Rachel fell to the floor and passed out. That stopped everything. Celeste ran to her grandmother, but Emma just stood there with little emotion.

"Grandma, wake up!" Celeste begged as she shook Rachel, in an attempt to bring her around. "Help me!" Celeste yelled to Emma. But Emma wasn't about to come to the aide of the one person she hated most.

"I'll be back tomorrow. You better be ready," said Emma as she literally stepped over Rachel and walked out the door and slammed it shut.

Celeste called the police to help her grandmother. It turned out that Rachel had only fainted. Emma arrived early the next morning and took Celeste away without even saying goodbye to her own mother.

Chapter 5

Hundreds of people were laughing and talking and running around in the county park. A banner was stretched across the park entrance. 'Welcome Louisiana Families 1958.' People were coming from everywhere. Families of all races and back-grounds walked, drove and came on buses. Some were well dressed in fine cars, and some were ragged and without shoes, but they all seemed excited and glad to be there. As the families entered the park, they gave the man at the gate some sort of invitation in exchange for a roll of tickets.

Three Black teenage boys entered the gate laughing and joking with each other. And even though they were all dressed poorly, somehow each of them seemed to have a style of his own. One of the boys, Walter Lee, was flirting with every woman he passed. Walter Lee was the youngest, shortest, cutest and boldest of the boys. His cut-off pants were so big they hung below his knees. His plaid shirt was missing its sleeves, but it didn't look too bad because he had a nice build for a small kid. Walter Lee had an obsession for big women. A beautiful dark-complexioned middle aged African woman strolled by with a fantastic sway to her large hips. This almost took Walter Lee's breath away. The other boys couldn't believe his actions. They laughed at him and walked on, pushing and shoving him as if to say he was crazy. But, he didn't care. He continued glancing back at the swaying hips.

An outdoor platform had been built in the corner of the park. A live band was jamming with Rhythm and Blues of the day. The platform was full of dancing couples causing the wooden floor to rock, jump and shake.

Emma was on top of the platform along with the others. Although overweight and overly made-up, she was a good-look-ing, middle-aged Creole woman. She was partying hard in her sexy red dress that flowed with every move of her extra-large hips. Her hair was what folk called 'good hair,' the kind of hair that wouldn't need a hot pressing comb.

In those days it was a good thing if you had light skin and 'good hair.' Anything that linked you with having some white blood was a plus. But that wasn't all it took to get a good old fashion Black man to turn his head. Women had to have large hips and big butts, and if she also had a light complexion and good hair, she was definitely one to be considered.

Emma knew how to use every bit of what she had to get what she wanted. She was easy on her feet despite her 200, well-proportioned pounds. She danced so much that the stress and strain on the floorboards beneath her seemed to come alive with every step she took as they shook to the beat of the music.

A crowd gathered around. Some of the women didn't like what they saw in their husbands' eyes. Emma, now known as 'Big Mamma' was the queen of Louisiana, and operated one of the most profitable brothels in the Southern States.

Gone were the thick long braids and the sullen face of a sensitive little orphaned girl. Also missing was the young and pretty eighteen-year-old who used to run around town with any man who had enough dollars to buy an hour of her time. Emma 'Big Mamma' Bouvier was now the wealthiest woman in the county.

The Black man Big Mamma was dancing with jumped up in the air and then landed down on the dance floor in a split, and then bounced right back up and continued with all of the latest moves with little or no effort. Big Mamma had some good moves too, and knew what to do with them. She could grind and roll her hip sockets so seductively they seemed to be detached from the rest of her body. The men folk were captivated.

Dancing next to her was her still-best friend Lena, who was

equally stunning. They were both drawing in the men. Lena still had her tiny waistline that complemented her large hips and beautiful long copper-colored legs. She rubbed Vaseline on them to make them shine like gold. Her sexy bright yellow dress against her flawless brown skin could not be missed. She was one of those women who didn't need good hair, or light skin, to attract the opposite sex. She was 'fine', and there wasn't a man in the county who didn't desire her, and not a woman who didn't envy her. After taking over the dance floor and having a good time, Lena & Big Mamma looked at each other and winked because they knew that they were working that crowd. Every man wanted to be with them, and every woman wanted to get rid of them.

Sheriff Tiddle, a middle-aged, pot bellied white man, was standing next to a little 80-year-old hillbilly-looking man with no teeth who was mesmerized by Big Mamma's moves. He and the sheriff gloated. Finally, the little hillbilly couldn't keep it to himself any longer. Big Mamma's moves got to him. "Go on, Big Mamma!"

Big Mamma threw him a kiss. The little man made a few dance moves that were hysterically uncoordinated and funny and then he nudged Sheriff Tiddle. The sheriff was obviously jealous of the kiss - that is, until Lena leaned over the edge of the platform and tried to coax him to join her and her partner on the stage. The sheriff blushed and said, "No." The crowd kept trying to get him to go, but he refused. "Ya'll know I can't dance."

"You know how to move when you want to," Lena embarrassed him.

The crowd laughed and whistled and applauded. The little hillbilly next to him punched him in the arm and praised him for what Lena had just said.

An extremely fast clicking sound was coming from the inside of a nearby tent. The clicks were going so fast that it was almost impossible to tell one click from another. A well-dressed young Creole man named Xavier was adding figures on an adding machine at an unbelievable pace as two other men, Pete Duplechain (Uncle Pete) and Chance Collier, watched in amazement. Uncle Pete was a clean-shaven 45-year-old man with good Creole features. He wasn't very tall, but he was secure with his height because he thought that every woman wanted him. The fast-talking, fast moving lover man had a woman in every county, so he said. And they all had children by him, so the people said.

Chance Collier was an uneducated 46-year-old White man who grew up out in the swamplands with the Creoles and Blacks. He was one of the few Americans who could care less about race or money. He didn't care about race because he was never taught the difference. He didn't care about money because he had never had any, and he never expected to get any. He could barely read, and he didn't care because he lived at home with his parents and five brothers. He just loved spending his time arguing and fighting with his best friend since grade school. The two of them only went to the 8th grade, and they weren't happy if they couldn't find anything to fight about.

Surrounded by mounds of invoices and papers, Xavier worked diligently. The music could still be heard outside the tent despite the continuous sound of the adding machine.

"Xavier, man, how you learn to do that stuff so fast?" Uncle Pete was amazed. "I went to Howard, Uncle Pete." (He kept clicking)

""Who's Howard?" Chance asked.

"Howard University, Mr. Chance. I'm an accountant."

"Howard University? Never heard of it. How many colored folks gon' to this university?"

"All of 'em." Xavier said proudly.

This made Uncle Pete proud too. But Chance's comment made him mad. Time for a good ole fight between Uncle Pete and Chance.

"You sure are ignorant, Chance Collier. Not knowin' that Howard University is a Negro college. Why, my nephew here..."

"Your nephew? That boy ain't your nephew!" Chance interrupted.

Uncle Pete hit back. "He ain't no boy neither! Besides, he is my nephew! And if it wasn't for me bringin' him in here to do these books, there wouldn't be no reunion!"

Chance couldn't let Pete have this one. "This picnic's been goin' on before Xavier ever saw a college. It's here to keep everybody together. That's what this reunion has always been about, and you don't have a damned thing to do with it!" Chance was mad. "We all volunteerin' our time. And right now, I'm volunteerin' to get the hell-outta-this-tent because you annoy me, Pete Duplechain."

Chance took his jacket and left the tent, but came right back and said, "By the way, I was told that half these kids that call you 'uncle' should be callin' you daddy!" Chance left again.

Uncle Pete yelled at him and talked fast trying to get it all out before Chance got out of his sight. "They just might be mine too. Every damned last one of 'em! Just cause the women round here want me - you can't take it! I done had more women then Carter's got liver-pills. I know it!"

Xavier couldn't keep from laughing at those two. But he didn't stop working. Uncle Pete was so mad he didn't know what to do.

"That is one White man that gets on my nerves!" Uncle Pete got up to leave.

Xavier stopped for a moment. "Where you goin', Uncle Pete?"

"I'm goin' to look for Walter Lee. Gotta keep him outta trouble. That boy loves women and ain't but 15 years old. I don't know where he gets it from."

"Who's Walter Lee?"

"My nephew!"

And with that, Uncle Pete stormed out of the tent. Xavier laughed so hard he almost knocked over his calculator and papers.

Meanwhile, the party outside went on. Big Mamma was dancing with a middle-aged, handsome White man. Lena had herself a young Creole boy. Every curve in both the women's bodies was swaying seductively to the down-home beat of the band. Everybody was moving with the music and loving it. Suddenly a young Black male about 15 years old jumped up on the platform and cut in on Big Mamma. This kid could really dance. Cleotus Leon "Clee" Strong was skinny, funny and danced like the wind. It was obvious that Clee came from a very poor family, but nobody cared because of his ability to entertain. His oversized pants, which probably belonged to his father, allowed him to move any way he wanted. Even his belt was too big, but the extra hole he punched in the middle of it kept his pants up.

Right after Big Mamma made one of her sexy moves, Uncle Pete's flirtatious nephew, Walter Lee, checked his pockets and yelled, "Damn, I've only got 60 cents left!"

The oldest and most conventional of the boys was Willie T. "T-Bone" Bradley, Walter Lee's cousin. T-Bone's hair was cut short on the sides, almost bald, with very little hair on top. T-Bone often wore white shirts buttoned up to the neck. His shirts were usually so small they looked like they were choking him. His pants never fit either. T-Bone's tennis shoes were the funniest thing. They were run down, but clean, and he had only one pair of black dress socks. He thought they would make the shoes look better, but the socks were stretched out of shape and tended to fall down on his skinny legs. He looked quite comical sometimes, but in a cute sort of way. Willie T. always tried to keep Walter Lee in line, but it didn't always work.

"I know you ain't gonna try gettin' some from that big old woman, Walter Lee." Willie T. asked. "Why you think they call her Big Mamma? She'll squash you like a bug! Besides, you gotta have a dollar, man."

"Well, squash me because I am gonna try it - and I know how much money I need to get it." Walter Lee bragged as he looked up at Big Mamma with desire. The other boys looked up at her with fear except for Bubba. He looked at her in disgust. "You better make sure you got an extra quarter to get some protection."

John Edward "Bubba" Bradley was seventeen years old, tall, broad-shouldered and slow-talking. Bubba wore cover-all jeans like the ones old men wear, probably because he was too big to fit anything else. Sometimes his shoulder strap would fall off his shoulder and for some reason he never attempted to pull it back up. That strap would hang down all day if nobody told him to put it back up on his shoulder. Bubba seldom wore a shirt. He probably didn't own one, and he seldom combed his hair. His excuse was that it was too thick, and it hurt. He swore one day he would shave it all off and just go bald like his father. He was a big boy, but he was sweet and gentle - most of the time. The only time he exercised his size was when he was teased. He didn't like to be teased. He probably would beat up a grizzly bear if it taunted him. The boys knew this, so they didn't mess with him too much.

A few feet away from the dance platform, beyond the cigarettes and beer, a wonderful aroma of authentic Creole cooking could be smelled. Families were lined up all the way around the food tents waiting to exchange tickets for food. Creole women and men dipped into large pots and loaded all types of Cajun dishes onto big paper plates.

Celeste was a tall healthy girl who loved to eat. She didn't know which part of her plate to dig into first. The smell of the jambalaya hit her nose, but the etouffee was begging to be chosen, so she started with the hush puppies. Two men standing in the line at the Gumbo tent spotted her and hunched each other. Celeste was concentrating so much on her food that she didn't notice the two men watching her. She stopped a moment at the dance platform to watch Big Mamma dance. Celeste's mouth dropped open when she saw how Big Mamma was moving. Celeste couldn't take seeing her own mother act this way, so she quickly walked away from the crowd toward the parking lot. The two men got out of line and followed her.

Big Mamma and Cleotus turned the stage into a one-act show. Everybody except a few jealous women screamed with delight. Big Mamma was in no way intimidated by this kid. The harder she danced the better she got. And the closer Cleotus got, the sexier she danced. Cleotus was a funny kid because he would get so embarrassed when Big Mamma got near him that he tried to get off the stage. She snatched him back and the crowd loved it as they applauded and whistled. Walter Lee, T-Bone and Bubba stood below the platform yelling support to their good friend, Cleotus. "You go, Clee!"

"Save some for me!" Walter Lee yelled. He was Big Mom's biggest admirer.

T-Bone was still trying to be his conservative self, but was so impressed by Cleotus's performance that he even tried a few steps while standing in place. However, his socks kept coming down so he stopped. Bubba's beat was totally off, but he was enjoying himself. Finally, Lena jumped in and took over. She was a bit easier on Cleotus. Lena danced well. Her sensuousness was a bit softer than Big Mom's was, but just as effective - even more so for some of the men. Lena definitely had her own fan club.

There weren't a lot of people in the parking lot area

because most of them had already arrived, so Celeste was able to find a secluded bench near the cars where she could pig-out in peace. She sat and ate, not realizing that she had been followed. The two men looked around to see if anybody was watching them. Celeste was oblivious to the trouble she was in for. Before the men approached her, they reached into their pockets. The Creole man pulled out a fake mustache and stuck it on his face. The Caucasian man pulled out a shabby dark wig and slapped it recklessly on his head.

By now Celeste had finished eating, and tossed the dirty paper platter and cup into a nearby trash can. She turned to walk back to the park grounds when the two men approached her. The Creole man spoke in such broken English dialect that it was difficult to understand him. "What you name, girl?"

"What do you want?" Celeste stood her ground The blood of her mother was about to kick in.

The two men said nothing else. They looked at her with lust and began circling her in a way that hindered her from walking away from them. As they circled, Celeste kept her eyes on them in case they tried something. After making sure that they couldn't be seen, the men started picking at her. At the same time, they were coasting her over toward a secluded spot by a truck. At first they pretended to be playing with her, but she knew better.

"I like 'em young and firm," the Caucasian man said.

"Yeah, me too." The Creole man had a really stupid laugh. He sounded like a hyena. The more they taunted her the more excited they got, and the angrier she got. Tension was high.

Finally, they stopped the stupid laugh and grabbed her by the arms and tried to force her behind the truck. At first, it was quite serious because it was obvious that these men were dangerous, but it became funny when the men realized that they couldn't do what they had intended, which was to simply throw Celeste to the ground and rape her. But Celeste was too strong. She fought back. Fearful, yet angry, she was determined to keep her feet on the ground. "Get off me!" she yelled.

Finally, the Creole man just got tired of struggling and punched her right in the face. She went down quickly. The fun was over. "Bitch!"

Blood flowed from Celeste's mouth. She was dazed, but not unconscious. The Creole man got on top of her as the Caucasian man held her down. The Creole man tried to remove her clothes, while at the same time, he started unzipping his pants, but Celeste began to struggle. "Hold her, dammit!"

They struggled. The Caucasian man was no match for Celeste. "I'm tryin'!" He yelled. "Shit, she's strong!"

One would think that Celeste would panic like most women, but she didn't. She was so mad she became the aggressor. Suddenly, she got one arm free and punched the Creole man right in the nose. He fell backward off of her. The Caucasian man was shocked. He let go of Celeste for a split second, which gave her time to jump up. With her pants hanging partially open and her blouse torn, she was ready to kill. She headed for the Caucasian man and caught him rising from the ground. She gave him a good punch in the mouth and then a double fisted bash to the side of his head. This man was out. The other man started to rise, wiping the flowing blood from his nose as Celeste quickly took care of him. She walked over to the plastic trash can that she had just tossed her food in and lifted it up, and plopped it over on the Creole man, leaving him stuck with the trash can over his head and trash all over his shoulders. He couldn't move and the other one was knocked out. They were a pitiful sight. Celeste walked away trying to make herself presentable.

Wandering aimlessly, Celeste found herself near the dance platform still trying to fix her clothes. As she passed the three boys, Bubba was the only one who noticed her. He was impressed with her, and she was taken by him, but because of her condition, she was ashamed, and walked quickly out of sight. Bubba watched as she disappeared into the crowd on the other side of the platform. He didn't mind the tattered clothes, and he couldn't see the other side of her face where she had a bloody lip. He just liked the person he saw, and he wanted to see more of her, but she left too fast.

Finally, the music stopped. Everybody applauded, yelled, screamed and whistled. Cleotus jumped off the stage and joined his three buddies. They took off to the others side of the park. Big Mamma and Lena laughed and bowed as if they had just finished performing in a grand burlesque show. Some of the women were upset with the way their husbands had been acting, but the more secure ones applauded right along with their men.

As Big Mamma and Lena took their final bows, Lena spotted Celeste approaching from the far side of the platform. She hunched Big Mamma and told her to look. By now, Celeste's eye had swollen almost shut and was about to turn purple, her lip was still a little bloody and her clothes looked a mess. If there was anybody there who didn't know that Celeste was Big Mamma's daughter, they were about to know it now. When Big Mamma saw Celeste her eyes turned a flaming red. If it were possible for steam to come out of her nose like an angry bull with a red flag being waved in from of him, it would have happened then. Big Mamma did not like what she saw, and was about to hurt somebody for doing this to her daughter.

Lena had learned her lesson a long time ago about interfering in Emma's business, so she knew to stay out of this. When Big Mamma got down off the platform, everybody else backed off too. They spread out around Celeste and watched in silence.

"What happened to you?" Big Mamma asked. She was furious.

Celeste was dazed and didn't have enough time to answer before she was bombarded with more questions.

"Do you hear me, girl? What happened to you? Who did this to you? Don't nobody touch my daughter. I'll kill 'im!"

Waiting in the gumbo line, Cleotus was curious about Walter Lee's desires. "Why you like that big ole woman, Walter Lee?"

Walter Lee gestured with his hands as if grabbing hold of something big and soft and wonderful. "I need something to hold on to, that's why. My Uncle Pete say it ain't no fun when you feel bones pokin' at you."

"Your uncle ought to know. He done tried everythin' from here to Shreveport."

The other boys laughed and smacked each other with approval on that statement. But Walter Lee didn't believe in going down so easily. "He ain't been nowhere your daddy ain't been."

"My mamma ain't big and fat, though." Cleotus didn't like for anybody to talk about his mother.

"But she's got a big ass!"

Okay, that did it. Walter Lee knew that he had overstepped his boundaries. Skinny little Cleotus was mad, and even though Walter Lee knew that he could whip Cleotus with one hand behind his back, he didn't want to have to do that, so he ran. Cleotus was so mad he chased him. The other boys followed, but they didn't really try to keep up.

"Cleotus ain't never gonna catch him." Bubba wasn't worried.

"And even if he did catch him, he couldn't do nothin' to him. Can't nobody hurt Walter Lee, especially Cleotus." T-Bone knew his cousin well.

Bubba didn't care what either of them did to each other. "I can whop Walter Lee, but Cleotus gets on my nerves too."

"Yeah, I guess you right, Bubba. You can whop most any-body in this here county."

"And if he talks about my mamma, I will hurt him."

"Walter Lee talks about everybody's mamma and daddy."

"That's because he ain't got none."

Walter Lee and Cleotus vanished from Bubba's and T-Bone's sight.

Bubba was always thought to be slow in the head, but sometimes he would come up with some pretty interesting thoughts. "I think Walter Lee's uncle he stayin' wit is got some-thin' to do with Walter Lee being the way he is. They say Uncle

Pete gets all the women. I think he's got a sex problem. I think that's what's wrong with Walter Lee."

T-Bone had different ideas. "The only problem Uncle Pete's got is he probably ain't getting' no women. If he was, he wouldn't have to talk about 'em so much. Everybody knows that people who talk about it all the time ain't getting' it."

"Yeah, I guess you right." They walked on.

Chapter 6

Loud country music, along with laughter and singing, was coming from inside Big Mamma's house. Cars and trucks were all over the yard, but one particular car cruised by as if searching for something. It was Sheriff Tiddle's police car, watching the parking lot. The door to the house opened, allowing cigarette smoke to escape, as two White men exited. Music from inside the house could be heard throughout the parking lot. The two men were yelling and laughing. It was obvious they had had a great time. After spotting the sheriff, they quieted down a bit, and got into their cars and drove off.

Sheriff Tiddle was steaming mad. He hated this situation because he had the hots for Big Mamma, himself. He watched as the door opened once again. Another man left. This one was good-looking. Big Mamma kissed him goodnight and pushed him out the door in fun. He staggered to his truck. She followed.

"You're beautiful, Honey." He hugged her so tight he almost lifted her off the ground.

"You drive careful, now, Mooney. I'll see you next week."

Mooney let her down gently, and kissed her once again. "If I find out anything about those bastards who attacked your daughter, I'll take care of 'em, you hear?"

"Thanks, Baby." Big Mamma blew him a kiss as he climbed in his oversized dump truck and drove off.

Because Tiddle was the sheriff, he had to keep a low profile. So he couldn't party with everybody else. He had to come to Big Mamma's house after hours, and she had warned him time after time that if he harassed her customers, she would cut him off. But he was so jealous of these men that he just couldn't help himself. He still found ways to get back at them. Sometimes he even resorted to flattening tires if they stayed too long.

The minute Big Mamma went back inside the house, the sheriff took off after Mooney with his red lights flashing. He didn't turn his siren on because he didn't want Big Mamma to know that he was out there harassing her customers again.

Big Mamma's house was filled with smoke, White men and sleazy prostitutes, and liquor bottles were everywhere. The country music, combined with a little down-home blues, sounded good, and the men were drunk. This was 'White Night.'

Wednesdays and Fridays were always set aside for the White men. All other nights except Sunday were for everybody else. Blacks, Creole, Asian, Spanish, and even the Geechee would drive down from as far north as the Carolinas, just for a good night out.

Celeste was wearing a modest little cotton dress that her grandmother had made from a Simplicity pattern. She still carried the scars from the attack in the park.

Celeste picked up the dirty glasses and went into the kitchen. She was amazingly oblivious to what was going on in that house. Big Mamma and the other sexy women didn't seem to faze her. She didn't understand this new world of people because Rachel had never told her anything like this existed. So, the best thing her little mind could do was to just 'do as she was told'. She cleaned up the dirty dishes, didn't talk to the men, and stayed out of the back rooms.

Some of the men whispered to each other about the possibility of trying out Celeste. They knew that that was a 'no-no,' but they watched her anyway because she had a dynamite figure for such a young girl. Her breasts were full and firm and her tiny waistline only accentuated her rounded hips. The little cotton dress didn't hide the fact that Celeste was definitely blossoming into a beautiful young woman. And even though her brain didn't seem to have a thinking cell in it, she had definitely inherited her mother's good looks. Lena wondered how Celeste could be in that environment and not know what was going on. But, the more she watched Celeste, the more she believed that Celeste must have chosen to just 'shut down' and not deal with the craziness.

Lena overheard some of the men's comments, and didn't like it one bit. "I know you'all ain't lost your minds. That girl is off-limits, and you know it!"

The men got quiet. They knew that Lena was right. Nobody wanted to go up against Big Mamma. Besides, they all knew that she was still looking for the men who hurt Celeste, and they didn't want to be suspected of doing anything like that.

* * * * *

Hiding in a shack back in the swampland were the two men who had attacked Celeste. The Creole man's name was Jacque Dupree, and the Caucasian man's name was Zebadiah Jones. Jacque was so frightened his hands wouldn't stop shaking long enough for him to light his cigarette. The matches kept going out before he could do it.

"How was I s'pose to know she was Big Mamma's daughter? I ain't been over dere in months. You been dere, why ain't you seant her?"

"I ain't been there!"

"You said you been there!"

"I lied! I ain't had no money to go nowheres." Zebadiah

tucked his head in shame. "Damn! We be in trouble! Can't be goin' back dere no time ever."

The thought of never again going to Big Mamma's place was devastating to both men.

"No more Big Mamma," Jacque moaned. "You think that girl would know us, Zebadiah?"

"You crazy? She saw my face and my hair. My wig went flyin', when she knocked the shit outta me."

The minute Zeb mentioned the wig Jacque realized that they had left the evidence behind. Jacque screamed, "Your wig! My mustache! We left 'em dere. Dey gonna find 'em! Oh, shit!"

Zeb wasn't worried because he never planned to go back there anyway. "I don't care what dey find. Dey can't pin it on us. How in da world can a hat and a mustache git somebody in trouble? All we got to say is we don't know who dey belong to. Don't be so dumb, Jacque!"

Jacque felt better. "Yeah, you right. Dey can't do nothin' to us just because of a stupid wig, or a mustache. I'm jumpy over nothin'."

Both men sat quietly for a long time. And then Jacque broke the silence. "Damn, she was strong!"

"I know what you mean. I don't want no more Creole women. I think I'm goin' back to White ones."

"I don't want none neither. Dey ain't never liked me noways, so maybe I should try some White ones too, or maybe Negroes."

"Negro the same as Creole," Zeb said.

"Don't let my cousins hear you say dat."

They sat quietly, thinking. Finally, Jacque broke the silence again with subtle laughter. "Kin you imagine if both dem women got hold to us? Dey so strong dey'd beat us stupid. I remember one time when Big Mamma got so mad at a man at her house, she whipped his tail all over her back yard. Dey had to take 'im to the hospital!" They laughed some more.

"Damn, I ain't even goin' to town no more!" Zebadiah said. They both continued laughing. "Can you believe we out here hidin' from two women?"

They both laughed so hard they thought their sides would split open.

Meanwhile, over at the fair grounds, Sheriff Tiddle was looking around for evidence. He had been there every day since the attack. He knew that if he could catch whoever did this, he would definitely be in good graces with Big Mamma. So far he had found the mangy wig and the false mustache.

Dirty blonde strands of hair were visible in the wig, so this confirmed Celeste's description of the White man, and the fake mustache had pulled a few whiskers out of Jacque's scruffy beard, so they had something to match up with the other description too. Sheriff Tiddle had good evidence, now all he had to do was find the men who matched it. Not many Creole and White men hung together in those parts, especially two men who would attack a little girl together. So, it didn't take long for the law to figure out that it must have been Jacque and Zebadiah, but nobody could find them anywhere.

Big Mamma was awakened by a telephone call. It was Sheriff Tiddle. "I got 'em," he yelled proudly.

"You got who?" Big Mamma asked. She wasn't quite awake.

"I got the two ass-holes that attacked your daughter," he bragged.

Emma got excited and angry at the same time as she sat up in bed. "I'll be right down there. I want to see those bastards."

Sheriff Tiddle suddenly realized that he had spoken too soon. "I don't have 'em here, but I got 'em." He immediately broke out in a cold sweat.

Emma was confused. "What do you mean, Tiddle?"

"I mean I got 'em! They just ain't here." Tiddle knew that he had better come up with the right answers right now or Big Mamma would be down there all over him, in front of his deputies in minutes.

"Well, where the hell are they then?" Emma asked.

"They're down in Gorman's Swamps," Tiddle said nervously. He knew at that moment that he shouldn't have called her until he had them both in custody. She was now going to make his life a living hell until they were behind bars.

* * * * *

The swamp was where Zeb grew up, so he knew every inch of the place, and could hide for years without ever being found. But Jacque soon got tired of those damp and gloomy woods.

"Man, I'm hungry," Jacque complained.

"Well, you can go up to the house for some food. My ma will heat somthin' up for you."

Jacque didn't want to tell Zeb that he didn't like his mother's cooking. Her main course was usually snake or some other type of reptile that Jacque didn't want to know about. "I'll git somthin' later. I really jus' wanna go home to my house."

"You ain't gonna be goin' dere for a long time."

"Do you think the law really be lookin' for us?"

"I know dey is. My cousin say dey is, but dey ain't comin' down here to the swamp. Dey scared my cousin say."

"Good. What you think Big Mamma would do to us if she come down here?" Jacque was seriously considering the consequences if he went back home.

"I don't know. After she finish whippin' on us, she probably git somebody else to beat our ass real good. We might not come out of it alive. Dey might hang us. I don't wanna think about it, myself, cause I ain't never goin' back dere."

* * * * *

Big Mamma had heard enough from Sheriff Tiddle. Nothing was making sense. "Is this some kinda joke, Tiddle? Because if it is, I'm gonna kill you."

"No, it's no joke. We got those two good-for-nothin' bums trapped down in the swamps."

"Ernest Tiddle, you ain't never been in the swamps in your whole life."

"I know that, but we know they're there. Beuford Hollis told us he saw 'em. They down there stayin' with Zebadiah's mother."

"Well, dammit, go after them!" Big Mamma was ready to

go herself.

Sheriff Tiddle tried to explain, "We got both exits blocked. Tiddle knew that there was no way you could block off a swamp, but he was trying his best to calm Big Mamma. "They can't get outta there without us catchin' em."

"So, you gonna wait until they come out?" Big Mamma asked sarcastically.

"That's right," Tiddle bragged.

Emma jumped up off her bed so fast the box springs went spastic. "You dumb son-of-a-bitch, they could stay in there forever! You take your sorry little ass down there and get 'em, you hear me?"

Tiddle didn't know what to say. The thought of his going into that swamp was a bit too much to handle. No way! It was time he tried to bargain with Big Mamma. But the minute he said, "But..." Emma stopped him. "But, my ass! You better go get 'em!"

Tiddle knew instantly that the argument was over with Big Mamma because if he continued, she would definitely cut off his weekly visits for who knows how long. So, scared half out of his wits, Tiddle quietly hung up the phone and proceeded to make arrangements for him and his men to enter Gorman's Swamps. All he could think about were the moss-covered trees filled with poisonous snakes, and the hungry alligators waiting to devour him. He also remembered that the marshland was named Gorman's Swamps because of the stories older people told about a man named Gorman who went into the swamp and never returned. One of the old townspeople claimed to have seen some giant green people take him away. And by the time the story was passed down through a couple of generations, it was said that the green people ate old man Gorman.

Sheriff Tiddle's legs shook so much he could hardly stand up, but he wasn't about to let Big Mamma know how scared he was.

* * * * *

Zebadiah's mother's cooking had really messed up Jacque's stomach. He had had diarrhea for a week. While the two were talking, Jacque kept squirming.

"What you keep movin' like dat for?" Zeb asked

"My butt hurts!"

"Your butt?"

"Yes, my butt, my ass!"

"What's wrong wit you ass?"

"I guess I got them hemorrhoid things."

"How you git somthin' like dat out here?"

"I guess it come from your ma's cookin'. I just keep shittin' and shittin' and can't stop. I done shit so much my butt-hole done turned inside out."

"You a damned liar sayin' dat dat come from my ma's cookin'! You don't see me shittin' all over the place, do you?"

"Yeah, well I ain't gonna find out if it's her, cause I'm goin' home! My ass hurt so bad, I feel like I been punked by a horse!"

"How you know how dat feel?"

"Don't be funny. I'm outta here." Jacque headed for the

shack that they were staying in, and got the little bit of clothes that he had brought with him. Zeb followed him, fussing. "I tell you, the law gonna git you!"

"I rather be got by dem, and face Big Mamma and her boys than to take any more bites from these damned blood suckin' mosquitoes! Dey done almost sucked all da blood outta my skin! I'm goin' home!"

With red lights flashing, three police cars merged on the main dirt road leading into Gorman's Swamps. One by one the cars fell in behind each other and slowly worked their way down the narrow bumpy road. Even though it was 3 o'clock in the afternoon, the density of the overgrown trees blocked out the sun, making the swampland every bit as scary as Tiddle had imagined.

Nobody spoke a word in all three cars. Tiddle was in the middle car, of course. He figured that he didn't want to be in the first car in case something approached them. Already short in stature, he looked even smaller as he slid down in the car seat in hopes that the 'green people' wouldn't see him.

Jacque threw his clothes in a burlap sack and set out through the foot-high marsh, heading for home, and talking up a storm to himself. "My feet been under water so long in dis here swamp, I know I done caught that athletic foot stuff the way my feet be itchin'."

Taking giant steps, Jacque quickly lifted one foot higher than the water and then down, and then the other one; step after step, trying desperately to escape that awful place, and still fussing with himself. "Why I wanted to mess wit a little ole teenage girl, I don't know. I ain't got the sense God gave me!"

Zeb watched as Jacque disappeared off in the distance. He was not about to follow him, and Jacque wasn't about to turn around and go back.

"Dey gonna be waitin' for you soon as you git dere!" Zeb yelled as he watched his long-time partner leave.

Suddenly the first police car hit a deep hole, and sure enough, it broke an axle. The men were outdone. Who was going to get out of the car and look at the damage? They were so far into the swamp that they could hear strange sounds that they had never heard before. The awful scream that must have been coming from some unknown swamp creature was almost too much to bear.

"What is the holdup?" Sheriff Tiddle asked. His driver could only see that the car in front of him had hit something, and was leaning heavily to the right. "I don't know what happened, but DuShon's car is definitely out of commission."

"What? What the hell you talkin' about, Bobby Lee?"

"I'm talkin' about DuShon's car. It ain't gonna run no more. And that's for sure."

Tiddle suddenly forgot about the green swamp monsters and jumped up to see what was going on. "Well, get that junk-heap outta the way so we can go on. I ain't about to be sittin' here when it gets dark."

Tiddle's driver didn't know what to do. He wasn't going to get out of the car to help anybody, and he didn't even know about the swamp people. But what he did know about were deadly snakes and alligators, and he didn't want any parts of that.

Jacque was tromping away through the marsh. His poor feet itched so badly he didn't know whether to scratch or keep walking. Finally, the itch hit him so hard he lifted his foot and reached down into the instep of his shoe in an attempt to scratch, and his finger didn't come out of his shoe fast enough and he lost his balance and fell right into the water.

Jacque hadn't realized that he had fallen in a spot full of leeches until he stood up and looked down and saw big black blood-sucking worms attached securely to every part of his body. He began screaming and running and trying his best to knock them off, but they were stuck to him as if to stay forever.

Gone was his burlap bag with all his belongings and he didn't care one bit. He just kept right on running and yelling for help. By now he had fallen so many times that green moss had attached itself to him as well. He was truly a mess, but he kept on running in a desperate attempt to get out of that God-forsaken place.

By now it was 4 o'clock in the afternoon and the sheriff's deputies had finally eased their way out of their cars to try and get Dushon's car started, but to no avail. And since the road was too narrow for them to get past the broken-down vehicle, they decided unanimously to turn around and go home. Not one of the men contested the idea, especially Tiddle, who never got out to help, but continuously stuck his head out the window to fuss at everybody else. "Alright, let's get this show on the road. Unfortunately, we can't proceed with this mission, boys, so we gotta turn around and go home." Tiddle was so happy he didn't know what to do, but he couldn't show it to his men.

Turning around in the narrow space provided was not easy.

The men had to slowly work their way through it because on each side of the rocky road was deep marshland, and one wrong move could be disastrous for both cars. So, the first car backed up slowly and began to turn as the second car did the same. Now this placed Sheriff Tiddle in the back vehicle, which didn't make him happy at all. "I think I need to be up front to help that idiot outta here."

So Tiddle's driver contacted the other vehicle with his two-way radio and told him to stop so that Tiddle could join him.

Because the sheriff was so anxious to get out of that place, he forgot for a brief moment to watch where he stepped when he got out of the car. The moment he put his foot down on the 'ground' it moved right from under him and he fell. The deputies heard Tiddle scream, but couldn't see him because he had slipped down the side of the embankment, and looking at him face to face was one of the biggest alligators one would ever want to see. Tiddle had stepped onto the back of an alligator when he got out of the car.

Well, life was definitely over for Tiddle, he thought. Except he hadn't banked on the fact that his men were not the cowards that he was, and they quickly ran the oversized beast away, and put the panicky and teary-eyed sheriff inside the front car and proceeded to complete the turn-around.

But just as the brave young men had gotten their cars almost headed back in the right direction, they saw something very strange and frightening moving aggressively across the swamp. This time they were scared too.

"Uh, Sheriff Tiddle, do you see what I see?" The driver asked.

Well, naturally Tiddle hadn't seen anything because he was too busy hugging the floor of the car. "I don't wanna see anythin' but home. So don't talk to me, just drive this piece of shit outta here right now or you're all fired!" Tiddle yelled.

But coming across the swamp was something that was so scary both drivers froze, and the two cars hit each other as the fast-moving green creature quickly approached.

After the obvious crash Tiddle decided to come out of hiding to see what was going on. By now the drivers were almost hysterical. Dushon, who was now a passenger in Tiddle's car, screamed. "Oh, Lord, we are goners now! Com'on, man push on the gas!" The driver tried desperately to move the car, but it was stuck in the mud.

Tiddle still hadn't seen what was coming. He was too busy yelling instructions at his men. "What the hell is the matter with you people? What does it take to get these cars outta here?"

Just then Tiddle saw what the men had been yelling about. And all he could do was stare, just like the others. Well, Tiddle thought he had finally seen it all. The green people really did exist, and one was headed right for him, with what appeared to be many arms lashing about in a menacing fashion.

"Oh, my sweet Jesus!" Tiddle exclaimed as the two-legged green monster got closer and closer, yelling something that the men couldn't understand.

Now all three cars were disabled, and the men were left with no other choice but to protect themselves from this unbelievable creature. Of course Tiddle was the first to draw his pistol and fire on the moving monster. And then the others began shooting, and the creature finally went down.

After numerous gunshots, the echoes traveled throughout the swampland. And then there was complete silence.

Little did the frightened men know that the fast approaching giant green monster was only Jacque Dupree, covered in dangling moss and blood-sucking leeches, running and screaming, begging them not to leave him behind.

Jacque didn't quite make it out of that terrible place, but he was now free of the hungry alligators, giant flying cockroaches, avaricious mosquitoes and leeches, and deadly snakes, because he was dead.

The echo of the gunshots traveled a long way because back in the swamp sat Zeb, crying because he knew that what he had just heard had to be the death of his closest friend and only buddy, Jacque.

Zebadiah never did come out of the marshland. It was said that he married one of those swamp White women and had about ten kids. All in all, he never visited the countryside or Big Mamma's place again. And Sheriff Tiddle and his boys never knew that they had killed Jacque Dupree because the alligators got to the body before the men could even think about going over to look at the creature that they thought they had destroyed.

Chapter 7

T-Bone's parents' small frame house left something to be desired, but it was clean and comfortable. The old wooden swing on the front porch squeaked as the boys sat and discussed sex. Cleotus was straight up with them saying that he was not ready for it. Walter Lee gave Cleotus a hard time, but T- Bone came to his defense. "Walter Lee, you ain't ready for this shit either. You just talkin' to be talkin'."

Walter Lee jumped up and reached in his pocket and dumped a handful of coins on the floor of the porch. "How's that?"

Bubba did not want to see the appearance of any money because this might mean that he really would have to go through with this whore house thing. "That's all fine and good, but what you gonna do with it?"

"What you think I'm gonna do with it? I'm goin' to Big Mamma's." Walter Lee said with confidence.

The boys laughed so hard that Walter Lee developed an attitude.

"What ya'll laughin' about? Ya'll just ain't got the guts to do it, that's all." Walter Lee picked up his scattered coins and started shoving them in his pocket.

T-Bone might have been scared, but he didn't want to be told that he was. "What you mean, we ain't got the guts? We'll do anythin' you do."

"Then do this."

"Do what?"

"You know what. Go with me to Big Mamma's. She takes young men on Saturdays between 12:00 and 2:00".

"You suppose to be 18 years old." T-Bone scolded. But in all sincerity, he was just stalling to keep from committing.

"I got that covered." Walter Lee took a fake driver's license out of his pocket. "I can get you one too. Besides, Big Mamma don't care how old you are. Uncle Pete says she don't look at no license or nothin'."

The boys weren't ready for this challenge. They began looking at each other hoping that the next one would come up with a better reason not to go.

Bubba spoke up. "We ain't got no money."

Walter Lee wouldn't accept 'no' for an answer. "T-Bone's got money. He's always got money. He'll loan it to you, won't you, T-Bone?"

T-Bone didn't want to answer that question, so he changed the subject. "I told you not to call me T-Bone no more. My name is Willie T. Besides, I got to get my ma somethin' with my money."

Bubba didn't want to go. "I ain't got no money, and I ain't borrowin' no money because I can't pay it back and I know it, so I ain't borrowin' it."

Cleotus stopped swinging and stood up. He always got real nervous when anybody talked about sex. "Me neither. Cleotus danced around nervously. "Besides that, I ain't goin'. My daddy and mamma would kill me!"

Bubba was still trying to avoid going. "Besides that, Sheriff Tiddle will lock us up." That was a good answer, but it didn't work. Walter Lee still insisted that they go with him.

T-Bone tried. "Besides that, I ain't loanin' nobody my money."

"You all scared! That's why." Walter Lee yelled.

Bubba didn't like being criticized even if it was true. "No it ain't! I'm older than you, so I know I ain't scared!"

Cleotus told the truth. "Well, I'm scared, but not of her. I'm scared of my daddy."

"That's just an excuse. You all chicken!" Walter yelled. The truth was that Walter Lee didn't want to go alone.

Finally, Bubba came up with a good stall. "Wait til' I get my own money. Then I'll go."

"Yeah, me too," Cleotus agreed.

"Like I said. You all chicken!" Walter Lee felt defeated, so he started walking away.

T-Bone was almost ready to go with him, but Walter Lee kept calling him 'chicken,' and that made T-Bone mad. "Don't call me no chicken, Walter Lee."

"You chicken, T-Bone." Walter Lee said.

The two cousins stood nose to nose.

"And don't call me T-Bone." T-Bone was mad.

Walter Lee knew that if he made T-Bone really mad it would be all over, so he tried another approach. "Tell you what? I won't call you T-Bone if you go with me."

T-Bone still hadn't made up his mind. "I ain't goin' without them."

"Well, they can go."

"I told you - I ain't borrowin' no money." Bubba was adamant.

"Me neither." Cleotus was just scared.

"Well, I ain't goin' without 'em." T-Bone stalled.

"Ya'll full-o-shit!" Walter Lee picked up his money and went home. The boys watched as Walter Lee ran off over the hill. They were horrified at the thought of doing this. They sat quietly, almost like zombies.

"What're we gonna do?" Bubba felt so bad.

"He called me chicken." T-Bone was devastated.

"I just ain't gonna do it." Cleotus didn't feel a thing.

"Me neither," Bubba confirmed it all.

"Then we're chicken," T-Bone said.

"I ain't chicken." Bubba didn't like being called chicken.

"Me neither." Cleotus could care less.

"We all chicken." T-Bone was right and Bubba knew it.

"... I know."

They all just stared out across the field. They were truly scared. The thought of having their first sexual experience was bad enough, but going to bed with this big old woman was much too much for them to think about.

Still troubled about being called chicken, Bubba set out to get his money. It was summer time and school was out, so he couldn't use his lunch money. So he set out to get a summer job. He was a big guy, so he decided to take on a man's job, and get fast money down at the fishing docks. He went to the Foreman and asked for work. The man took one look at him and gave it to him. Bubba smiled and got to work immediately, loading crates of fish.

Even though Cleotus was positive he was not going through with this sex thing, he still decided to make a little money in case his buddies didn't get enough for themselves. So, he went to town and started to dance for money on one of the street corners. He chose a place where he was sure his parents wouldn't see him. And sure enough, his parents didn't come, and the people tossed him the money he needed.

Willie T-Bone was pretty sure he would support his cousin.

He had always backed Walter Lee. Besides, he thought he could handle this. He took on a job at the church tutoring old people. The odds of his making money were slim, but he was willing to try.

"You're gonna be ready to read this Bible by yourself before long, Mrs. Green."

"Bless you, son. God bless you."

Mrs. Green handed him a quarter! He accepted it with one of the biggest smiles you ever saw.

Bubba had a very profitable weekend. He made five dollars and some change. He figured he had gotten enough money for everybody now, so nobody was going to get out of this. If it ended up that he had to go, everybody was going to go. He put his money in his dresser drawer and went to sleep.

* * * * *

Walter Lee was shooting basketballs into his makeshift hoop. He was obviously troubled because he kept missing the basket.

In the far distance he could see his three friends approaching. Walter Lee saw them and pretended like he didn't care. He continued trying to make baskets. As they got closer, he played harder. They walked up to him and waited for him to acknowledge them. Finally he did. And without words, they reached into their pockets and pulled out handfuls of coins. Bubba had dollars. Willie T-Bone decided to handle this. "Tomorrow's Saturday, ain't it?"

Walter Lee didn't want them to know how excited he was,

so he smiled and shot his basketball straight through the hoop without even touching the rim.

Saturday finally came. The boys walked down the road all dressed up. They looked like they had all had baths and were going to church. Their hair was combed and their shoes were clean. Walter Lee was excited. He couldn't even walk a straight line. He ran from one of the boys to the other, teasing and joking with them.

Walter Lee ran up to Willie T. and flipped down the top of his pants, exposing the top half of his underwear, which was bright red.

"Look, man." Walter Lee was getting on T-Bone's nerves real bad.

"Look at what?" T-Bone asked.

"My draws! They're red! And silk! Sexy, huh?"

With his pants half off, he tried to put on a cool walk. The boys thought he looked ridiculous, and he did. But Walter Lee didn't think so. "My Uncle Pete gave 'em to me. He said they excite women."

"Your uncle couldn't excite a cat." Bubba was annoyed too.

"Yeah? Well, we'll see about that. When I get in there and turn on my charm, Big Mamma might close down the place. She might not want to see any of you chumps."

"You the chump! Actin' like your life depends on this sex thing." Bubba was scared beyond belief. He lagged behind.

Walter Lee circled back to him. "No, you got it wrong. Sex is dependin' on me. Cause I'm gonna write a new book on the subject." Walter Lee ran out into the middle of the road and jumped up and down yelling... "I'm gonna change the world!"

In the distance a car approached slowly. The boys didn't see it coming. Walter Lee continued teasing his friends. The car slowly pulled up alongside them. It was Sheriff Tiddle. The boys were startled when he spoke. "What you boys doin' way out here?"

Bubba, Cleotus and Willie T. just about jumped out of their skin. Walter Lee remained calm. He had had encounters with the law before. T-Bone tried to handle it calmly. "Just walkin', Sir."

Sheriff had his suspicions. He knew that kids went to Big Mamma's on Saturdays, and these boys were close to her house.

"There ain't much on this road. Where ya'll goin?"

Walter Lee and Cleotus answered at the same time, only they both said something different.

Walter Lee said, "...Fishin'."

Cleotus said, "...Store."

T-Bone tried to clean it up. "...The fishin' store."

"Ain't no store down this here road." Sheriff Tiddle knew better.

T-Bone continued to make up stuff. "Oh, we call it 'the store.' It's where we get our worms out the ground for fishin'. We got a special place."

"Yeah - it's special." Cleotus was nervous.

Bubba said nothing. He was almost hidden on the other side of the boys. Sheriff Tiddle noticed and looked over at him and asked, "What's wrong with you, boy?"

They hunched Bubba to make him respond. "Huh? Oh,

nothin', Sir."

"You actin' like you hidin' somethin'."

"No Sir. I'm just not feelin' too well this mornin'."

The boys are so close to the house they can almost see it in the distance. And at this point during the conversation each boy has looked in that direction at least once. Sheriff Tiddle was sure that they were headed for Big Mamma's, and he was not going to let them do it. "Well, I suppose if you ain't feelin' too well ya'll better go on home."

Walter Lee gave Bubba the mean eye.

"Oh, I ain't feelin' that bad, Sir."

"You boys look awfully clean to be goin' fishin'."

Walter Lee stepped out in front. "Oh, we do this sometimes. We dress up, pretendin'."

"Pretendin' what?"

They couldn't think of anything. Panic suddenly set in. And then T-Bone saved them again. ..."Pretendin' we goin' to the big city to go to the fishin' store."

Well, the boys knew that that was just about the dumbest answer anybody could give. They looked at T-Bone like they could kill him.

"That's about the dumbest thing I ever heard." Sheriff Tiddle said.

"We do dumb things sometimes." Bubba was referring to this trip to Big Mamma's. He rolled his eyes at Walter Lee.

"You boys wouldn't be going over to Big Mamma's place, by chance, would you?" The sheriff asked.

"Big who?" T-Bone played dumb.

"Oh, no Sir! My daddy would kill me." Cleotus jumped around with nervous energy.

"I know your Daddy, too. And I don't think you want me to tell him I seen you over here, do you?"

"Oh, no Sir, I don't!" Cleotus almost became unglued.

"I told you where we goin'." Walter Lee said as he stood his ground.

"Yeah, we goin' fishin', Cleotus threw in nervously. "And we goin' after fishin' worms." T-Bone did the same, only he wasn't quite as adamant as Walter Lee was.

Bubba tried to be convincing too. "Yeah, the worms."

"You goin' to Big Mamma's, Sheriff Tiddle?" Walter Lee decided to turn this around on the sheriff. The other boys couldn't believe that he said that.

"What? No! Boy, you gettin' smart with me?"

"Oh no, Sir. I just asked cause I see your car over there alot."

Well, the boys were sure they had had it now. Guilt was written all over the sheriff's face.

"I just keep my eye on everything in this here county, that's all. And now I'm gonna keep my eye on you."

"Well, you and Mrs. Tiddle have a good day, Sir, cause I see her every now and agin' in town. I will shore nuff tell her what a good job you do for folks aroun' here by spendin' so much time over at Big Mamma's - keepin' your eye on things."

The sheriff knew that Walter was threatening him with telling his wife, and he didn't like it, but he couldn't do anything about it. "I'm gonna be watchin' you, boy. Now, get on away from here! Now!"

The boys answered together. "Yessir!" And then they took off across the field. Bubba was so mad. "Forgit this shit!"

"Walter Lee, you about to get us all in trouble." Willie T's nerves were shot.

"Ah, he can't do nothin' to us. My Uncle Pete told me that Big Mamma won't let him hurt nobody cause if he did, she wouldn't let him come over no more."

All four boys headed into the woods to get off the road.

"You mean he goes there too?" Cleotus asked. He couldn't believe it.

"Yep, and so does your daddy." Walter said.

"Walter Lee, leave that boy alone." T-Bone defends everybody.

"Your daddy's been there too, T-Bone... and Bubba, your da..."

Bubba grabbed Walter Lee up by his neck and started choking him.

"Don't you say it. I'll beat your ass all over this field."

Cleotus jumped around like a little squirrel. "Beat his ass, Bubba! Kick his ass!"

Walter Lee could barely breathe. "...Put me down, Bubba."

Bubba pulled his shirt collar tighter. "Well, don't you say it. I don had enough of you."

"I ain't gonna say nothin'. Walter Lee choked.

You got us in this shit, so you better keep your mouth shut about everythin' that gets on my nerves. I'm sick of your teasin'."

"Okay, okay."

"You play too much, Walter Lee." T-Bone tried his best to put a stop to all this.

"I ain't playin'. Bubba's daddy does go..."

Bubba hit Walter Lee so hard he landed on the ground and didn't move.

"Bubba, are you crazy, man?" T-Bone bent down to help Walter Lee.

"We shut him up that time, Bubba!" Cleotus was ecstatic.

Bubba felt bad for hitting Walter Lee. "I didn't mean to hit him so hard."

T-Bone tried to wake Walter Lee up. Cleotus was still jumping around nervous. "Maybe now we can go home now. My daddy's..."

"If I hear about how your daddy is goin' to kill you one more time, I'm gonna deck you!" T-Bone was tired of Cleotus too.

Bubba picked Walter Lee up. "You all right, Walter Lee?"

"Yeah." Walter Lee said as he brushed himself off.

Bubba looked out of the woods to see if the sheriff was still there. T-Bone tried to look too. "Can you see Tiddle?"

"No, but I've changed my mind. I ain't goin'." Bubba was out.

That's all Cleotus needed. "Me neither."

"We've come this far, I'm about ready to go ahead and get this thing over with," T-Bone said.

"That's my man!" Walter Lee suddenly felt better. Bubba didn't. "Forgit that. I'm outta here."

Bubba attempted to leave, but T-Bone and Walter Lee grabbed him. Bubba was a big guy and it took a lot for the boys to hold him. Walter Lee was upset. "But you agreed!"

"I take it back."

And of course Cleotus had to say it..."My daddy will kill me!"

Bubba just couldn't take it anymore. "Big Mamma's gonna kill you when she sits on your shit! Lordy, Lord, I'm scared of all that woman."

Bubba was determined to get out of this. He broke away from Walter Lee, but T-Bone held on to his leg.

"Let go of me!" Bubba yelled.

As usual T-Bone was the only halfway cool and calm one in the group. "No, we goin' through with this like we promised."

Bubba was leaving regardless.

"Get him, Walter Lee!" T-Bone yelled.

Walter Lee took a diving leap on to Bubba's back and knocked him down. T-Bone didn't let go of his leg. "Get his other leg, Clee!"

Cleotus was so skinny he was not about to tackle this bear's leg. He looked at the leg for a long time trying to figure out how to grab it. Bubba was furious. "Get off me, fool! I don't want no man on top of me! I ain't no faggot! Get off of me!" Bubba fought, but the boys fought harder. They held on.

T-Bone instructed them as he struggled to hold on. "Get his leg, Clee!"

All Cleotus could see was this gigantic leg flinging and twisting. Cleotus couldn't do this. So, he went around to the front of Bubba and grabbed Bubba's head, but even Bubba's head was too strong for him. Bubba tried to throw Cleotus by bucking like a bull, but Clee gave him a lock on his neck that Bubba just couldn't shake. Cleotus rode Bubba like a bronco in a rodeo. All this time Walter Lee was on Bubba's back and T-Bone had a lock on one of his legs. Walter Lee and Cleotus almost bumped heads because they were so close to each other. Finally, Bubba conceded, and they all dropped to the ground. Bubba was exhausted. "Okay, I give." Everybody was so tired they couldn't speak.

It was time to head out for Big Mamma's once again. When the boys got back to the road they looked both ways for the sheriff. The rest of the way was well out in the open, so they could no longer remain hidden in the woods. However, this time they were going to make sure to watch for Sheriff Tiddle.

Well, there it was! Big Mamma's house! Right across the open field. The boys stopped and stared. Walter Lee was excited, but nervous. "There it is!"

Bubba was not happy. "Shit!"

T-Bone was still in control. "Well, we're here now. Might as well go on over there."

Bubba cursed. "Fuck!"

Walter Lee chimed in. "That's just what we're gonna do."

Cleotus was about to have a fit. "Shut up, Walter Lee! What if we catch somethin'?"

This was the first thing Cleotus said that made sense. Everybody stopped to think for a moment.

"I gave you somethin' to use. You brought it, didn't you?" Walter Lee asked.

Cleotus looked in his pocket and pulled out a condom. He held it as if it was going to bite him. "Yeah."

The other boys checked their pockets. Finally, they proceeded across the open field, which felt like it was ten miles long. Walter Lee led the group. Willie T-Bone caught up to him. Bubba and Cleotus fell behind, looking around to see if anybody was watching. All was clear.

The boys finally approached the back of the house. They proceeded cautiously around to the side, and were shocked at what they saw. Alongside the house was a long bench, and at least eight boys were sitting on it, waiting in line to see Big Mamma. There was about five Blacks, two Caucasians, and one Chinese. The Chinese boy looked out of place because he was so small, but he was the most calm and seemed to be the most secure about being there.

There was only enough room for one of the boys to sit. They all looked at that one seat. Nobody said a word. Suddenly, a loud bang was heard. The four boys almost jumped out of their skin, but they quickly saw that it was only the front door slamming as a young boy exited and headed towards the road. After a moment Celeste came out. Her scars were still visible. Her big coverall jeans were not attractive. Nobody would ever expect someone who looked like this to be working at a place like this. Bubba was surprised to see her. He stared at her. He said nothing, just sat back, baffled at her presence. Celeste didn't notice him. She just yelled..."Next!"

The next boy jumped up and went inside, and everybody slid over. This left enough room for two more. Walter Lee took charge. "Who wants to sit?"

In a split second everybody replied, "Not me!"

"Well, you gotta sit sometime!" Walter Lee sat first. There was room for one more. Bubba pushed T-Bone to the front.

"Don't push me, Bubba."

"Go head, T-Bone."

"Okay, but don't push me."

By now Cleotus had moved behind everybody. He was not about to go next. T-Bone sat. Walter Lee turned to the boy next to him. "How you doin?"

"I'm cool."

"Tell me, what's it like in there? I don't know. I ain't been before."

The Chinese boy joined in on the conversation. "It's good! I go flee times." He held up three fingers. "She is vely good."

Suddenly the door banged again and the boy who had just gone in was out. T-Bone jumped. "Damn, that was fast!"

The Chinese boy responded. "When its' good, its' vely fast." He smiled from ear to ear. The boys looked at each other.

Walter Lee started bragging. "I ain't gonna be fast. I get 5 minutes for my dollar and I'm takin' it." (Proudly) "I can handle it." Walter Lee noticed that the Chinese boy had a bag with him.

"What you got in that bag?" Walter asked.

"Coke."

"Coca Cola?"

"Yes."

"Why? There ain't no time for that, is it?"

"You bring Coke, she give you extra."

Each time Celeste came out Bubba stared. He was really fascinated by her, but he was not about to go in that house. She yelled once again... "Next!"

The next boy went in, leaving room for another. Bubba turned around and snatched Cleotus up and placed him in front. But in a flash Cleotus whipped back around behind Bubba like a squirrel. He did it so fast that Bubba didn't realize what had happened.

"What you doin, Cleotus?"

"Leave me alone, Bubba."

Bubba tried to use his muscle again. He picked Cleotus up and placed him in front again and then pushed him down on the bench, but Cleotus was quick. In a flash, he was up again and back behind Bubba. This squirrel moved fast!

"Boy, you makin' me mad," Bubba growled.

Cleotus said nothing. He was not about to be next. Walter Lee couldn't take these two any more. "Will you two stoppit? Bubba, sit down!"

Bubba rolled his eyes at Cleotus and sat reluctantly. Bubba turned to Walter Lee and T-Bone. "That boy is gonna make me hurt him one of these days."

The door opened this time without a bang. The boy came out almost at the same time as Celeste. "Next."

The boys moved down again and now there was room for Cleotus, but after the boys moved over and looked up, Cleotus was gone! All that they saw was the back of him racing across the field toward home. Cleotus never looked back. Bubba was so angry he didn't know what to do. "I'm gonna get him for this."

Celeste was sitting and reading her book. Suddenly the door to Big Mamma's room burst open. The kid was running out with his pants halfway down. Celeste took the book from her face and watched him without emotion. The kid was in total fear. "I can't do it! I ain't never seen nothin' that look like that!"

The kid tried to get out the door, but couldn't open it and hold his pants up at the same time. Celeste calmly got up and opened the door for him and bit on her apple as she watched him run across the front yard, still holding up his pants.

The boys got closer and closer to the front, and Bubba was getting more and more nervous. One young man was extremely over weight, and sweating uncontrollably. He constantly wiped his face with his shirt. This was his first time too. Another kid sat with a paper bag in his hand and a smile on his face.

Walter Lee was next. He was a little nervous, but he had decided that he could handle whatever was coming.

* * * * *

Walter Lee was finally in the house. Celeste told him to wait in the living room. After checking out this moderately furnished home, Walter Lee started to sit, but just as he was about to bend his knees he bounced right back up because Celeste came out to get him. "Go on in." Celeste sat with her fruit and book and started to read. Walter Lee was nervous, but ready. He went down the hall and stopped at the door and knocked. When he heard Big Mamma's voice, he suddenly got even more nervous.

"Get in here, boy," she yelled. "You only got five minutes,"

Walter Lee slowly opened the door and was shocked at what he saw. Everything was decorated in red and black lace. The oversized room had an oversized bed with oversized mirrors everywhere. And Big Mamma was lying up in her bed in a gigantic red, sheer nightie. One of her thighs was as big as Walter Lee's whole body. He had never seen anything like that in his life. Big Mamma was sipping on a Coke and eating peanuts. Walter Lee stood there, not knowing what to do next. Big Mamma didn't even look at him. She had become so callous to what she was doing that she felt absolutely no guilt for messing with these young boys.

"You never done this before, boy?"

"No ma'am."

"Get those clothes off."

Big Mamma got up and went into the bathroom. While she was gone Walter Lee removed his clothes, but kept his shirt in front of him. She came back with a porcelain pitcher full of hot water. Walter Lee didn't know what to expect. His knees were actually knocking. She poured the water into a matching porcelain bowl and then dumped bath oil in it and swished it around, causing lots of suds. She then dropped a large sponge in the water and made more suds.

"Come over here and stand on this towel." Big Mamma had done this so much; she knew exactly what to do with each new face that came along. And this was definitely one of the easy ones.

Walter Lee approached cautiously, still holding on to his

shirt. Big Mamma quickly snatched away the shirt and went to work.

Staring in the boy's eyes, she slowly squeezed the sponge in the soapy water and then placed it on his shoulder allowing the warm water to trickle down his body and over his butt and gently down the front. The soapy water slowly rolled through his sparse pubic hair and rested on his penis, causing it to become so erect you could stand a chair on it. Walter Lee's eyes got big as saucers. He liked it. And when she took the sponge beneath his waist, the anticipation was too much for him. He ejaculated before she barely got past his navel. Walter Lee was in ecstasy. "Oh-h-h!" He made a ridiculous sound, and was finished in seconds, before she even touched him where it counts.

Outside the house T-Bone and Bubba were next. The line was almost as long as it was when they arrived. They waited for Walter Lee to come out. It looked as if he really did take his five minutes. Little did they know that on his way out, he stalled for time by staying in the rest room. He wanted them to believe that he did what he promised - took his five minutes.

The door swung open, and Walter Lee came out with a wide grin on his face. He waved at the guys and started walking across the field to the road with his chest stuck out in pride. He faked it well. The boys thought he had done something great. They looked at each other in amazement. Celeste came out and yelled, "Next."

T-Bone slowly got up and entered the house. Well, Bubba was about to die. He started talking to himself. "I gotta go through with this shit. I got to."

The boy next to him looked at him like he was crazy.

"What you lookin' at?" Bubba asked.

"I ain't been able to figure it out."

Bubba didn't like that statement. If looks could kill, this boy would definitely have been dead. "You ready to get hit in the mouth."

"If you think I'm gonna choose fightin' you over goin' inside, you crazy." The boy replied.

There was nothing Bubba could do. He had run out of excuses, he had to do it.

Inside Big Mamma's bedroom T-Bone was having the time of his life. He was riding Big Mamma like a wild bronco. And the look on his face was priceless. He was in shock and ecstasy at the same time. "Whoa-a-a-a-a."

Big Mamma was lying on her back and humping T-Bone up and down with little effort. She was so big, and T-Bone was so skinny, that it didn't take much to toss him around. And, at the same time, she was eating her peanuts and enjoying her usual Coca-Cola. She could care less about this boy whose yelling became so loud that he sounded like the siren on a fire engine as he came. Suddenly, Big Mamma realized that her Coke bottle was empty. "Time's up, baby. You gotta go."

She slammed the bottle down and flipped T-Bone on to the floor with his pants down around one ankle. He tried to stand up right away, but couldn't coordinate himself to do so. Big Mamma got off the bed and went to her private bathroom. T-Bone tried to get his pants on but couldn't. His legs seemed to be made of rubber.

Bubba, waiting nervously, saw Celeste helping T-Bone out of the house. Once she got him outside, she let go of him and went back in the house. His rubbery legs made it impossible to walk correctly. He looked like a cartoon. He made his way over to the bench.

"Lord, she sat on him!" Bubba yelled.

The other boys laughed. Well, this was enough for Bubba. He knew that he was not going in there now. "I'm takin' you home." Bubba grabbed at T-Bone, but T-Bone pulled away.

"No, (puff puff) you goin' in there! I'll wait for you right here." T-Bone said.

"But..."

"But nothin'. Don't be no chicken, Bubba. I did it and (puff puff) I feel great!"

"Man, I can't do this."

The boy next to him was really enjoying Bubba's fears.

"What's the matter? You a sissy?" The boy laughed.

That was the wrong thing to say. Bubba was about ready to fight for real now, but Celeste came out of the house and yelled, "Next!"

"Oh, Lordy, Lord." Bubba knew he had to go through with this. But when he approached Celeste something happened. Celeste seemed to be looking at Bubba the way he had been looking at her at the park. It was love at first sight. Bubba liked her so much; he literally tucked his head like a little kid before entering. For that brief moment he thought about how much he would have liked to have been coming there to court Celeste instead of wanting to hump her mother. He was so busy being apprehensive about all of this; he didn't notice how much Celeste was staring at him all the way into the house.

Once they got inside she told Bubba to wait. She went in to her mother's room and stayed quite a while. Bubba didn't know what to think. He glanced down the hall, but saw nobody. What is going on? Finally, Celeste came out and said, "Sit down." She went back outside and yelled..."Next!"

Well, T-Bone was really confused now. "Where is Bubba?" All the boys looked at each other. The next boy went inside, concerned. T-Bone stopped Celeste. "Where is my friend, Bubba?"

"He said for you to go home."

Inside the house the other boy was surprised to see Bubba sitting in the living room, and Bubba was equally surprised to see him going right by him and down the hall to Big Mamma's room. Celeste came back to Bubba, and with very little expression said, "You comin' with me."

She grabbed him and they went in a different direction. Celeste had chosen Bubba for herself.

A week later T-Bone and Walter Lee were lying up on T-Bone's front porch thinking about how good it had been last Saturday. Walter Lee flipped a dime on the porch floor. It was all the money he had, so he knew he wouldn't be going back to see Big Mamma any time soon. He was pretty depressed. "Have you seen Cleotus?"

T-Bone looked toward Cleotus's house. "That punk."

Even though Walter Lee was feeling pretty low, he started to laugh when he thought about Cleotus. "Did you see that fool run? He went over that hill like a jack-rabbit with a fox on his tail."

They both laughed. Walter Lee could hardly speak he was laughing so hard. "If Bubba coulda' caught Clee, he woulda' beat him within a inch of his life."

"Wasn't nobody gonna catch Clee."

Walter Lee was laughing so hard he was crying. "But just the look on Bubba's face when he realized Clee was gone. I ain't never seen Bubba that mad. Where is Bubba anyway?"

T-Bone was curious about Bubba too. "After that girl chose Bubba, I ain't seen him since. I think he's still there."

Walter Lee finally stopped laughing. He was starting to get a little jealous of Bubba. "I called his house and his mother said she ain't seen him but once since Saturday. She said he told her he got a summer job."

"Yeah, we know what that job is."

Walter Lee was depressed again. "Damn, he's lucky."

T-Bone wanted to keep the moment as uplifting as possible. He never could stand to see his little cousin unhappy, so he decided to talk about what he knew Walter Lee was thinking about all this time. "Damn, that was good, wasn't it?"

Walter Lee agreed. "Yeah. You got any money, T-Bone?"

"What's my name?"

"Oh, I forgot. You got any money, Willie T.?"

"No."

Walter Lee was about to get mad at T-Bone. He knew that T-Bone always kept money. T-Bone explained... "I told you that money was for somethin' for my mother. Sunday is her birthday, and don't nothin' come before my mother, you know that."

"Of course I know that. She's my aunt, remember, fool? But you the smart one, always teachin' somebody to read and stuff. Ain't you got no jobs comin' up at the church or nothin'?"

"They don't pay me to teach readin' at the church. I volunteer for that. Too many of the old folks can't even read their bibles. That's what keeps us down. We stay dumb and on Welfare."

Walter Lee didn't like that statement. "You always makin' talk about people you don't know nothin' about. My Uncle Pete might be on Welfare, but he ain't dumb. I get tired of hearin' that kind of talk from you. Makes me wanna kill myself sooner."

"I wasn't talkin' about your Uncle Pete, and I didn't say people on welfare are dumb. I said it keeps us down. It makes us too comfortable to do anythin' with ourselves."

Walter Lee was still defensive. "That don't make no sense."

T- Bone explained. "That little ole check makes us lazy. As long as we know it's comin' we don't have to try to do better."

Walter Lee didn't agree. "As long as I know it's coming, I feel great! I don't know what you talkin' about. Uncle Pete say Welfare ain't nothin' to be ashamed of."

T-Bone agreed, but... "We don't have to be ashamed. It's just not something that will help us get ahead. We get use to it and like it. So, it keeps us down."

"Uncle Pete say there are more White folks on welfare than Negroes."

"My daddy say that too, but that don't make it all right for everybody to do it. White or Colored. Just for some that can't help themselves."

Walter Lee kept bringing this back to himself and his Uncle Pete. "I ain't never gonna amount to nothin' no way. Might as well take the check."

T-Bone had a lot of pride. "My daddy won't take no check, and I ain't gonna take no check. I'm gonna be somebody."

Walter Lee seemed to be going back into his depression. His whole attitude about life was complete hopelessness. "I ain't gonna amount to nothin' and I know it. I ain't never had nothin', and ain't gonna have nothin'. I ain't got no parents, I ain't got no money, I ain't got ..."

T-Bone saw a slight tear in one of Walter Lee's eyes, and he didn't like that. "You got me and Bubba and Cleotus, and Uncle Pete and my mother and my daddy. That's a whole lot of people."

Walter Lee sat in deep thought. There was a long moment of silence. T-Bone waited for him to speak again, but he didn't. He wasn't feeling good about himself and T-Bone knew it, so he tried to comfort Walter Lee again. "You know you can always come live here at my house. My mother told you that so many times."

"I know, but I have to take care of Uncle Pete. He needs me." Walter Lee replied.

And like a flash of light, Walter Lee was finished with serious talk. He had suddenly decided to change the subject. It was strange how he did it, but he quickly got back to his old self again. It must have felt safer to be cocky and self-centered. There was no pain or heartache. There were no thoughts of the past or the future. "All I need right now is a dollar for Big Mamma. I just want to be back up there on that big red bed with that big yellow woman for another 5 minutes."

T-Bone was ready to change the conversation too. "You know you didn't last no 5 minutes."

"You wanna bet? She didn't want to let me go! I'm tellin' you she was moaning!" They both laughed.

Things were better now. T-Bone could feel it. Walter Lee got serious. "Listen, what did Bubba do with that five dollars he had?"

"I don't know."

"Maybe we could go over to his house and find it."

T-Bone didn't like that idea, so he came up with his own, "Maybe we could go to the fishin' dock and make our own five dollars."

They thought for a moment about the hard work involved, and then they both replied, "Nah-h-h."

So they both started thinking again. Finally, Walter Lee came up with another idea. "Wait a minute. Didn't Cleotus have his own money?"

"Yeah?"

"Well, he didn't use it, right?"

"Right."

Walter Lee always tried to talk T-Bone into stuff, and usually succeeded. "And the odds of him using it any time soon is slim, right?"

T-Bone wasn't convinced. "Maybe."

"Maybe my ass. That little punk don't plan on ever goin' back to Big Mamma's. You can bet on that."

"So?"

"So, he's got a dollar!" And we need it!" Walter Lee won. So they headed for Cleotus's house.

Cleotus was sitting in his room reading a book entitled 'Your First Sexual Experience.' He heard a knock on his door and immediately attempted to hide the book beneath his pillow. However, his father entered before he got it secure, so it fell to the floor beside the bed. His father didn't notice the book at first. He was mainly concerned with finding out what Cleotus's problem was. "Got a minute?"

"Yessir."

Cleotus was nervous because he didn't have time to hide the book properly. His father finally noticed, but said nothing about it. He sat on the bed with Cleotus. "Your mother tells me that you've been in your room for almost a week. That's not like you."

"I just haven't been feelin' too good."

"You need a doctor?"

"No."

"You need advice?"

Cleotus tucked his head and said nothing. His father asked more questions. "Sex?"

Okay, Cleotus was ready to talk. "You said that I would know when I'm ready."

"Right."

"Well, I'm - scared."

"You're 15 years old. You got plenty of time."

That answer was not good enough for Cleotus. "...But everybody has done it but me."

His father was patient and caring. "I know what you mean, but trust me, Junior, you got time."

Cleotus was quiet. He was not happy. His father got up to leave, but he couldn't help commenting on the book. "Maybe by the time you finish that book you readin' you'll be ready."

The father smiled and left. Cleotus was so embarrassed. He just sat there holding his head in his hands. After a while, Cleotus heard a knock at the door downstairs. He heard his father go to the door and answer it, and then call to him. "Cleotus, your friends are down here."

Cleotus couldn't believe what his father had just said. He couldn't believe that they had come over to his house! He didn't know what to do. He was so embarrassed. He started his nervous jumping, and fast squirrel-like action moves again. His father called to him again. "Junior, did you hear me?"

Cleotus didn't answer. He hid his book under the mattress and then sat on it.

"Cleotus Murphy!" Mr. Murphy yelled.

Cleotus thought to himself "Why doesn't he stop callin' me?" Cleotus went to his door and opened it a little and tried to whisper to his father. "I'm not here."

His father didn't hear him. So Cleotus tried to say it again, only a little louder this time. "Cleotus is not at home!"

His father still couldn't hear him. "What did you say?"

"Well, that's about it," he thought. "Now they know I'm here." He closed his door in desperation. "What am I going to do now?" he thought to himself.

His father decided to ignore Cleotus's ridiculous actions, and send T-Bone and Walter Lee upstairs. "I'm sendin' them up to you."

Cleotus looked around his room for a place to hide. He tried to get under his bed, but there was too much junk under there. He tried to push everything aside, but there just wasn't enough room - or time. They were coming in the door while his scrambling feet were still exposed from beneath the bed. The moment Cleotus heard the door open he stopped his feet from moving. I guess he figured if he didn't move a muscle, they wouldn't notice him. Of course the boys saw his feet right off. And of course Walter Lee loved this. "Com'on out, Clee. We see you under that bed."

Cleotus refused to move. He talked to the boys from underneath the bed. "Get outta my room!"

T-Bone found this to be so funny, he almost laughed out loud. "That ain't no way to treat us after runnin' away like that."

Cleotus stayed under the bed. He wasn't about to show his face. "I ain't comin' out, so you might as well go home."

Walter Lee kicked one of Cleotus' feet. "We ain't goin' nowhere, so you might as well come out."

T-Bone kicked the other foot. "Com'on, man. We want to ask you about somethin'. We ain't gonna tease you. We promise. So, come on out Clee."

Walter Lee was trying hard not to be impatient. "Yeah,

com'on out. We promise. We wanna ask you somethin'."

Cleotus stayed there. "Ask me from here, Walter Lee."

"What did you do with that dollar?" Walter Lee asked as he and T-Bone waited for an answer, but Cleotus said nothing.

"What did you do with it, Clee? We need it."

"I ain't got it," Cleotus finally responded. " I spent it."

T-Bone knew this meant a lot to Walter Lee, so he tried to get the money for his cousin.

"You ain't spent no money, Cleotus, and you know it."

"Well, I ain't got it, now get outta my room." Cleotus was being stubborn.

Walter Lee's patience was wearing thin. "Well, I guess there's only one thing we can do."

T-Bone knew that Walter Lee was getting mad. "What's that?"

"Look for it. It's probably under his mattress."

Well, Cleotus knew that the book on sex was under there, so he wasn't about to allow that to happen. He scrambled out from under the bed, and the squirrel was up and at it before they could take two steps. He said, "Okay, okay I got it - and you can have it."

The boys were surprised at his sudden willingness. He came out and without looking at them went over to his closet and took the money out of a box in his closet and gave it to them. Walter Lee smiled. "Hey, thanks, man."

T-Bone was surprised. "Yeah, thanks Clee."

However, Walter Lee wasn't finished. "But I wonder what's

under that mattress that's so important that you came out from under that bed so fast."

Walter Lee started for the mattress and Cleotus jumped in front of him and sat on his bed over the book. "If you don't get outta my room, I will tell my daddy what you did and why you're here!"

Well, the boys didn't want that to happen, so they reluctantly agreed to leave. Walter Lee was still curious though. He had a way of not backing down from anything he had a mind to do, so it really bothered him that he could not see what was underneath that mattress. "I don't know about you, man. You hidin' somethin' from us."

"You know you better get outta my room," Cleotus said. He was mad at them now, and would really have resorted to fighting both of them, or telling his father about what they did if that's what it took to keep them away from his mattress.

"Yeah, we goin'," Walter Lee said.

"See you around, Clee." T-Bone was not about to fight with Cleotus.

They left, and Cleotus slammed his door shut and breathed a big sigh of relief.

Walter Lee knocked on the front door of Bubba's house while T-Bone stood back. You could already smell the aroma of southern fried chicken, black-eyed peas and corn bread. Bubba's family was definitely not Creole. This was the true aroma of honest-to-goodness, good ole Mississippi soul food. Whenever Walter Lee would get tired of Uncle Pete's cooking and wanted a really good meal, he would come over to Bubba's house. Mrs. Bradley always enjoyed feeding Bubba's friends. But right now food was not what was on Walter Lee's mind.

Mrs. Bradley came to the door. She was a big lady like Bubba, and you could tell that she was a very respectable church-going woman. You could also tell that she ate a lot of her own cooking.

Walter Lee could really be charming when he wanted to be. "Hello, Mrs. Bradley. Is Bubba at home?"

"No, we ain't seen Bubba for a couple of days. He said he took a job over in Shreveport for a little while. He said he'll be home on Sunday in time for church though. I don't know what possessed that boy to do such a thing. He knows we can provide for him." The boys just listened while she expressed her dismay.

"There ain't nothin' I can think of that boy needin' that bad."

Walter Lee and T-Bone looked at each other. T-Bone was very polite. "Well, thank you, ma'am. Tell Bubba we were lookin' for him."

As the boys left, T-Bone was about to walk down the walkway, but Walter Lee pulled him quickly to the side of the house.

"What are you doin', Walter Lee?"

"Com'on with me." T-Bone knew instantly that Walter Lee was up to something. They went to the side of the house and Walter Lee looked into Bubba's bedroom window. This did not sit well with T-Bone.

"Man, if you don't get away from there! We gonna get in trouble sure-enough," T-Bone snapped.

Walter Lee didn't say anything more. The window to

Bubba's room was open a little, so Walter Lee quietly climbed inside. T-Bone was having a natural fit. He started to leave the premises. He was so mad at Walter Lee he didn't know what to do. He walked away fussing. "I ain't gonna be no parts of this! Man, you must be addicted to pussy!"

Chapter 8

Bubba was laid up in Celeste's bed. He was worn out and extremely quiet. Celeste entered with a large tray of food. "Here. You gotta keep your energy up."

Well, Bubba was completely exhausted. "I ain't really hungry, Celeste. You feed me every two hours."

"That's because I love you."

"I thought I ate a lot, but I ain't never seen nobody eat like this."

"I do."

You could tell that if Celeste kept eating like this, it wouldn't be too long before she would start looking just like her mother. But, in Bubba's eyes, she would still be the most beautiful woman he would ever lay eyes on.

All he could think about was how pretty Celeste was, and how she seemed much too innocent to be in this bedroom with him. However, he also knew that he was about as out of place as she was. And for the first time he realized what Cleotus meant when he said that his daddy would kill him if he knew about them coming here. This was definitely shameful, but Bubba didn't want to leave. He really liked his new girlfriend.

She put the tray down on the nightstand, and instead of going back and completely closing the door, she proceeded to eat. Bubba watched her and almost got sick to his stomach. He looked around the cheaply decorated room and wondered what he was doing there. Celeste watched him looking around, but didn't know what he was thinking. "I'm gonna be gettin' me some mirrors like mamma's pretty soon."

Bubba sat up. He couldn't believe what he had just heard. He almost started to studder. "W-what? Why? For What? Who decided that?"

"Big Mamma. She say I'm ready now."

"Ready for what?" Bubba instantly broke out in a sweat. He was so mad he could explode.

"I don't know. But she say I'm ready, so it must be so."

Bubba grabbed Celeste by the arms real tight, "Celeste, do you understand what your mamma really does?"

"Yes. And you're hurtin' me!" Celeste cried.

Bubba loosened his grip. "What do you think she does?"

"She counsels men." Celeste said as she rubbed her bruised arm. But Bubba wasn't finished with the conversation.

"Counsels?" He yelled.

"Yes." Celeste insisted.

"What do you think that means?" Bubba asked.

"It mean she helps men with their problems."

"And what do you think their problems are?"

"Different things. Mamma say everybody is different and wants different things." Celeste was getting tired of the questions, but Bubba wasn't tired of asking them. He was determined to make her understand what she was about to do.

"Did she tell you what the different things are?" Bubba was almost sarcastic.

"She say some of them have wives that don't like them the way they want to be liked."

Bubba stared at Celeste to see if she truly did not understand the situation she was in. He continued to ask questions. "And how are their wives suppose to like 'em?"

"I don't really know, but she say I'm gonna learn everythin' Friday night. It's White men's night. She say I'm ready now that you came here. She said you gotta go home tomorrow so she can teach me what you can't."

Bubba was ready to explode. Celeste was dumber than he was! He thought to himself.

"She say you and me are like the blind leadin' the blind."

Celeste tried to hug Bubba, but he pushed her away. "You ain't gonna be doin' what you mamma doin'."

"But Mamma say I'm ready to counsel. She say I'm ready to start my career."

Bubba couldn't take this. The thought of those men putting their hands all over Celeste was too much for him to take. "Career? You sixteen years old, Celeste!"

"Mamma say she was sixteen when she got her career started."

Bubba tried to calm down. "Celeste, this ain't no career. Your mamma is a whore!"

"A what?" Celeste was ready to fight.

"A whore! A prostitute - a whore! She's havin' sex with all those men!" Bubba wanted it to sink in to her brain, but it didn't.

"My mamma ain't no whore!" Celeste yelled.

Bubba tried to hold down his voice so that Big Mamma wouldn't hear. "Like Hell, she ain't. I was goin' in there to have sex with her myself! You gotta know that, Celeste. Ain't nobody that dumb!"

"You callin' me dumb?" Celeste was ready to put him out!

"No. No, I didn't mean it that way. I'm sorry. But, how did you know what to do with me if you ain't seen your mamma doin' it?"

"I was just lovin' you, Bubba." She was so innocent - and dumb!

"Yeah, shit, you sure was lovin' me, and that's a fact. And I was lovin' it, but who taught you?"

"Nobody. Big Mamma told me that nature would tell me

what to do when it's time."

"You went in there and told your ma that you wanted me?" Bubba just couldn't get over this girl.

"I sure did." She tried to hug him, but he wasn't finished talking.

"Tell me somethin'. Why were you so messed up at the County Fair?" Bubba asked.

"Messed up?" She didn't want to talk about it.

"Yeah, messed up. I saw you. Your clothes were all ragged and you were real dirty. Now, why?"

"Some men jumped me." Celeste replied.

Bubba was mad all over again. "Jumped you? But, why? You mean they raped you?"

"They tried, but didn't." Celeste hesitated a moment, and then continued. "They couldn't."

Bubba didn't understand what she meant. "They couldn't? What do you mean they couldn't? Who was it? Why couldn't they?"

"I don't know who they were, and they couldn't because I beat 'em up."

Bubba scratched his head. "You what? You beat two men up?" Celeste looked down at her hands like a shy little girl.

"Yes." She confessed. "My grandma taught me how to protect myself. She said men folk think with what's in their pants, not with what's in their head, so when their thinkin' ain't right, kick 'em in their pants."

Bubba loved her so much. "You ain't so dumb. And I'm

sorry I said that."

He hugged and kissed her, and tried to make everything all right. "They probably jumped you because they know about your mamma."

Celeste started to pull away because he was talking about her mother again, but she didn't because she knew inside that he meant well. Or, maybe she already knew deep down inside the truth about her mother but refused to face the facts. Bubba continued to question. "Didn't the kids at school tease you about her or nothin'? Everybody round here knows that she's a wh..." Bubba stopped. That was not the right thing to say, so he cleaned it up. "...Everybody knows what she does."

"No, I lived with my grandma until this summer. I went to school in Georgia. Big Mamma say I'm finished with school now. I gotta work."

Well, that did it. Bubba was mad all over again. So Celeste tried to explain more in hopes to make him understand.

"My grandma didn't want me to come here. She said I could be somethin' special if I wanted to. She said I should go to college."

"Your Grandma is smart."

"She told me that a Black man invented the red-light. You know, the stop-light?"

Bubba was amazed. "Yeah?"

"Yeah. She said White folks won't tell you about things like that. That's why you gotta read. She told me how a Colored man invented Blood Plasma, and then he died because he couldn't get no Plasma because he was a Negro."

"Damn!" Bubba was fascinated with this information.

"Grandma was mad at Mamma for takin' me."

Bubba held on to her. "She should'a been mad. But, I'm glad you came."

There was a brief moment of silence, and then Bubba asked the question he had wanted to ask for some time. "Was this really your first time?"

"Yes," Celeste confessed.

Bubba was so in love he didn't know what to do. He had found himself somebody he could really be happy with. He looked at her innocence and then thought about the situation she was in. She was about to become a prostitute for her mother!

Neither Celeste nor Bubba noticed a large shadow approaching the small opening in the doorway. They had forgotten to go back and close the door after Celeste brought the food in.

Bubba stared into Celeste's eyes and then kissed her lightly on the lips as Big Mamma watched through the crack in the door. And then the young couple began to slowly touch each other. Bubba stared at Celeste's small firm breasts as he slowly leaned forward, gently kissing each of them - one at a time. And he continued to watch as her beautiful pale brown nipples quickly rose to the occasion anxiously awaiting the next gentle lick. He thought they were the most beautiful things he had ever seen in his life. And she knew that she had found her true story book prince.

Emotionless, Big Mamma continued to watch the two young people express their love for each other. She couldn't see everything that was going on in the room because the door was only slightly ajar, and she knew that it would probably squeak if she tried to open it wider. But she was fascinated by the innocence of the young couple's lovemaking and wanted to see more, so she stood there and watched, unnoticed. And even though she knew in her heart that this was truly a beautiful sight, she would never admit to it because it was the one thing that she had always wanted but never had - true and passionate love.

Chapter 9

T-Bone was sitting on his front porch swinging and reading. Walter Lee stepped up on the porch quietly. T-Bone knew he was there, but didn't want to be bothered. He continued reading. Walter Lee tried to talk to him even though he knew that T-Bone was mad at him. "Hey."

T-Bone never could ignore Walter Lee too long. "Hey." He replied dryly. T-Bone kept his eyes on his book. Walter Lee sat down on the wooden floor of the porch next to Willie T. "I guess you ain't talkin' to me."

Walter Lee threw his magazine down. "Man, you broke into somebody's house!" The thought of what Walter Lee had done made Willie T.'s blood boil all over again. "No, you broke into your friend's house!"

"I know. I wasn't thinkin'. Anyway, I didn't take anythin'. I came right out after you left me."

T-Bone was glad to hear that. It made him feel a little better about the whole thing. He finally started to warm up a little after Walter Lee said that. But he still wanted to fuss at Walter Lee. "When you want somethin' that bad, it ain't worth havin'. You make me shame that you're my cousin!"

Normally T-Bone protected Walter Lee, but now he was really disappointed in him. Walter Lee remained quiet. What could he say? Nothing. So, T-Bone started again. "All our lives you been impatient and ain't never cared about nobody's feelins but your own. It's always been about what you need and what you want, and I always went along with it because it was you. Daddy said part of growin' up is when you can care about somebody besides yourself."

Walter Lee remained quiet as long as he could. "I know, T-Bone. But somethin' gets inside of me that say 'I want it now' and then I can't see nothin' else but that. I guess I ain't growed up yet."

"Well, there must be alot to growin' up, and we can't do it all at once. But you shoulda' started by now. Daddy said that a real man should be able to see past his own nose."

"What's that mean?" Walter didn't understand. T-Bone wasn't exactly sure himself, but he tried to explain. "I think it means we got a lot of time ahead of us for sex and shit. It felt good, sure enough, and I want more right now sure enough, but I got sense enough to know that I ain't got no money and I'm gonna have to wait til I get some. And I will get some. You can bet on that. But I definitely don't plan on stealin' it."

Walter Lee started feeling a little ashamed of what he had done. "You think I ought to give Cleotus back his dollar I got?"

They both thought for a moment and then responded simultaneously. "Nah-h-h."

T-Bone was glad Walter Lee had come over. This made them both feel a little better about the incident. They were glad to make peace with each other. T-Bone assured Walter Lee that if Bubba came home for the weekend, they would ask him for the money.

On Friday afternoon Bubba and Celeste were still in bed. Bubba noticed something different about Celeste. "You know, you ain't ate since breakfast."

"I know."

"Ain't you hungry?" He was concerned.

"No. I guess eatin' was always there to fill that space that needed fillin'."

Bubba put a little smile on his face. He knew what Celeste was talking about. "What's fillin' it now?"

And sure enough, she came through with the correct answer. "You." They embraced.

Big Mamma and Lena were having coffee at the kitchen

table. Lena was very upset with her best friend. "Emma, you can't put that child to work."

Big Mamma seemed to have absolutely no problems with her decision. "She's sixteen years old now."

"I know it, but she's - she's..." Lena didn't know how to say what she wanted to say. Big Mamma wanted her to spit out whatever it was. "She's what?"

"Emma, she's not too bright."

Big Mamma didn't like that statement. Lena knew that it hadn't come out right so she attempted to clean it up. "Don't get me wrong. She's a sweet girl, but... well, she's so innocent."

That was a better word. Lena was relieved that she came up with it. But, she still wasn't getting away with it that easy.

"Innocent? Big Mamma asked. "Do you know where she is right now?"

Lena knew, and even though she didn't approve of it either, she still defended Celeste.

"I know, but they're in love."

Big Mamma got up from the table to get more coffee. She seemed to be doing this in order to avoid eye contact with Lena. "Love, my behine. They don't know what love is."

Lena pleaded as best she could. She knew how stubborn Big Mamma could be. "You gonna make that girl hate you, Emma Bouvier."

Big Mamma was determined to do what she wanted. "Once she get started, she'll like it. I liked it."

"Well, now, I don't think you can compare that child with you. Seems like you been likin' it since you were born."

The women chuckled. Lena continued. "I remember when your mamma caught you and that little boy behine the sofa. You were ten years old! Girl, you were working that little boy."

Lena got up from her chair and started moving back and forth seductively, mocking Emma, never noticing that Big Mamma was troubled by her comments. This was slowly bringing back some pretty bad memories for Emma. She tried to cover up her instant flash of pain by going along with the conversation. "Yeah, you were suppose to be my look-out."

"Your mamma came too fast."

"I remember, you pe-e-ed all over yourself when she walked in." Big Mamma pointed a teasing finger at Lena.

"I sure did." Lena admits. Big Mamma tried to continue with the conversation. "Girl, she whipped my butt so hard I couldn't sit down for a week."

"What ever happened to that boy?"

"The next day, I pulled my panties down and showed him the bruises and I told him he'd better kiss my boo-boos." Big Mamma bent over and rubbed where she had gotten spanked. "And he ran home crying. He told his mama and she told mine, and then they moved outta town."

Lena laughed, but Big Mamma started to remember what had really happened after that. She started to remember how Marcus acted when he found out. She started to remember how he beat her until the blood oozed from her little legs. And then he beat her mother. Emma lit a cigarette to calm her nerves. "You always been bad, Emma," Lena said as she sipped on her coffee. She didn't realize that Big Mamma had stopped laughing. She hadn't noticed that Big Mamma's eyes were so swollen with tears that one blink would cause endless teardrops to roll down her face. But Big Mamma would never allow anybody to see her cry. Not even her best friend, Lena, who unknowingly rattled on and on about the one thing that Big Mamma hated to deal with the most, her past.

Big Mamma's back was turned as she puffed on her cigarette. Her eyes had become completely bloodshot. The old memories had caused her blood pressure to shoot up. Those memories brought back all the pain and frustration of the past, leaving her angry all over again. This was the Big Mamma that everybody in town knew not to cross. This was the Big Mamma that Lena knew when to leave alone. Big Mamma put her cigarette out and finally spoke, in a low and despicable tone, which was Lena's signal to shut up.

"And Celeste is going to be just like me." Emma said.

Lena stopped laughing. And even though she would normally have left the house when Big Mamma got like this, her heart still went out to Celeste, so she decided not to walk away from this discussion without trying to talk some sense into her angry sidekick. "You gonna lose your name-sake and only child, Emma Celestine Bouvier." Lena lit a cigarette for both herself and Emma.

Whenever Lena would try to get Big Mamma to listen, she always talked to her quietly and called her by her full name. She picked that up from Emma's mother. But none of this was helping. Big Mamma got up out of her seat and proceeded to walk out of the kitchen as if she had suddenly become hypnotized by a key word, and was headed out to do something very sinister.

She only replied with, "Wanna bet?" And then Big Mamma stopped and turned back to Lena and stared at her with the coldest eyes one could imagine. Whenever she got mad she had a way of crimping a cigarette in the corner of her mouth and puffing on it without hands. Lena had seen Emma angry many times, but never had she seen her like this. "I don't remember you coming to see me when I was in all those foster homes. I don't remember you even writin' to me. Marcus wasn't mad because I was playin' with that boy. He was jealous because I was practicin' what he had showed me! And my mamma knew what Marcus was doin' to me, and she did nothin' about it! Nothin'!" Emma's cigarette was down to a butt that fast, so she quickly put it out and took another.

Big Mamma paced back and forth as Lena sat and listened. Lena wanted so badly to stop Emma from talking so that she could explain that she had been only a small child herself, and was told that Emma had gone away to live with relatives, but she knew not to interrupt Big Mamma when she was mad.

Emma leaned over the table and stared at Lena. The smoke from her cigarette curled up Lena's nose, but Emma didn't move it, and Lena didn't pull away from it. She just stared back at Emma and said nothing.

Emma continued. "Where was everybody when he was sneakin' in my room at night smellin' like cheap wine, runnin' his filthy hands up my nightgown and into my shit? And my mother had the nerve to say she was 'sorry?' And then expected me to hug her and say all was forgiven, when all the time she would be sittin' in the next room listening to me cry, 'No, Marcus, that hurts' - over and over - night after night? And final-

123

ly, on my tenth birthday he started fuckin' me for real. I guess all those other years when he used his fingers he was tryin' to stretch me so that his shit could fit in mine. And when he finally did it he messed my guts up so bad, the doctors thought I would never have kids. My mother told them that a stranger did it, and then she took me right back home to him. Fuck no, I wasn't forgiven' her! If she died tomorrow, I would dance on her grave! I don't forgive nobody for what I went through! Nobody!"

This was making Lena's stomach turn.

Emma continued, "It took a lot of years to figure out why that bastard sent me away, but I finally understood it. The police was about to get his ass. That little boy's family was out for blood. And if anybody woulda' examined me they woulda' found out just how messed up my shit was, and any fool coulda' figured out who did to me. He just didn't want to go to jail, that's all." Emma put her cigarette out with such force that she broke the ashtray.

"Yeah, I went and got my daughter from that bitch this summer, and if she had tried to stop me, I woulda' stomped her blue like Marcus did. I don't care if she is old now. She took Celeste from me when I was eighteen years old, and that has ate at me and ate at me. Now I got my daughter back, and she'll do what I say!"

Big Mamma stormed out of the room leaving Lena stunned at what had been said. Lena could have never imagined in all her years of life that something so awful had happened to her best friend. No wonder she was always so angry.

Celeste and Bubba heard a loud knock and then the door burst open. Big Mamma was ready for business. "Celeste, I want to talk to you." But, being Emma's true daughter, Celeste was also ready to give back whatever was about to be dished out. She got up and left the room. Bubba sat quietly even though he wanted so badly to go in there and defend Celeste against this woman.

In the living room Big Mamma stood holding a bright red flowered sundress. Her eyes were completely bloodshot, but this didn't affect Celeste. She stared right into them, waiting to hear what her mother had to say. Big Mamma stared back. "Celeste, Honey, I told you your boyfriend's got to go."

Celeste still wanted what Bubba said to be a lie, but all of her instincts told her that it must be true, so she fought back. She was determined to make her mother tell her what all this was about. "But, why can't he stay and wait in my room til I'm finished trainin' tonight?"

"Because we are gonna be needin' your room. I bought this dress for you."

Celeste didn't like the skimpy little dress. She refused to take it. Big Mamma insisted. "Put it on after your bath."

"Why we got to use my room? Ain't I'm gonna be watchin' you? And why do I have to wear that dress? I don't even like all those wild colors and skinny straps. And we don't need nobody in my room for nothin'!"

Big Mamma was getting angrier. She shoved the dress at Celeste again. "Yes we do."

Celeste pushed it back at her. "No we don't!"

Big Mamma reached over and grabbed her hand and slammed the dress in it and made her take it. "You listen to me, girl. You are sixteen years old now, and a whole lot of men will pay a lot of money for you. So you better get in there and get rid of that worthless piece of shit, change them sheets, take a bath, comb your hair, and douche because you are goin' to work tonight!"

As Big Mamma was about to leave, she had another thought. She took one long draw on her cigarette and then turned with a completely different look on her face. It was a look of complete disdain. "As a matter-of-fact, I think we need to do somethin' to your hair first."

Celeste cried and threw the dress to the floor. Her pain and anguish was so deep that she couldn't make a noise. She just stared at Big Mamma. "It's all true what Bubba say. You ain't nothin' but a whore!"

Big Mamma slapped her hard across the face, picked the dress up off the floor and threw it at Celeste and stormed out. Celeste looked around at that tacky red room and that tacky red dress and thought about the possibility of her doing this for the rest of her life and she cried and cried and cried.

Bubba sat on the side of the bed, worried, when suddenly the door burst open and Big Mamma entered with fire in her eyes.

"Pack your shit and get the fuck outta my house!"

126

Chapter 10

Loud country music filled Big Mamma's house. The combination of dim red lights and dense cigarette smoke in the living room made it almost impossible to see, but one didn't need much light to notice the tall skinny white man sitting in the corner with yellow false teeth that moved up and down when he laughed. Straddling his lap was one of Big Mamma's whores. The equally thin White woman with long stringy blonde hair didn't seem to mind the teeth at all. It wasn't the teeth she was concentrating on as her hand slid slowly and methodically up and down inside the deeply aroused man's pants, at the same time resting her tongue in his ear. This man was in heaven while she sat on his lap and caressed and teased him with her long pale legs wrapped around his waist. Finally, he reached in his pocket and pulled out what the woman was waiting for, a big wad of money, at which time they got up and headed through the thick haze of smoke to the extra bedroom down the back hall.

The party was hot and steamy that night, and it wasn't because of the humidity. Ever since Celeste moved in, Big Mamma had made sure that everybody behaved in her presence. Nothing other than singing, dancing, drinking and a few sneaky rubs took place out in the open. Anybody who wanted to pay for sex had to go to the proper room with the woman of his choice. And Big Mamma always took her men to her bedroom. But now Celeste was about to be introduced to the real deal because all bans had been lifted, and folks were wild again. The old brothel was back in business.

Word was that Big Mamma was going to turn Celeste out that night, so everybody showed up. The wealthier men had already put up their bids, and those who could not afford it wanted to be there if for no other reason than to witness the big event. Men drove in from all parts of the southern states with plenty of money in their pockets, all hoping to be the first to taste this fresh young meat.

Xavier was in one of the back rooms counting the cash. He knew about the situation with Celeste but had been so well trained by Big Mamma to 'mind his own business' that he was determined to focus only on the money. This job paid well, and he wasn't about to blow it by interfering, even though he could hear Celeste's painful cries filtering threw the corridor walls.

Some of the locals had already lost their money at the poker table in the kitchen. A few of the others spent their small earnings in the walk-in pantry where drugs were stashed. It was a standing joke about how Big Mamma always kept her pantry 'full.' She had everything anybody needed, from marijuana to cocaine. But most of the men held on to their money that night. They wanted this little girl real bad.

Celeste squatted in the corner of her room crying uncontrollably. The thick black eye makeup and bright orange rouge ran down her face, making her look like a melting porcelain doll. She was so frightened she couldn't move.

Lena sat quietly in the kitchen. She just couldn't get with the party because she could hear Celeste crying through the wall. She wanted so badly to go in there and comfort the frightened teenager, but she feared the consequences from Big Mamma. She considered going home, but couldn't leave Celeste there alone. She kept thinking about what she might do if one of those greasy old men headed for Celeste's room "How could Emma do this to her only child?" Lena thought.

Lena had never had kids of her own, so Big Mamma allowed her to be Celeste's belated Godmother, and Lena truly loved the responsibility, so this hurt her deeply. This also contradicted Big Mamma's reaction when Celeste was attacked in the park. Nothing made sense to Lena. So she sat in the kitchen and wept silently in the corner and watched as the inebriated men on the other side of the room played cards and made jokes about the 'coming out' of the kid. And at the same time she was listening to Celeste cry her heart out on the other side of the wall. Lena wanted so badly to go over to that table and turn it upside-down, and put every one of them out. But it wouldn't have done any good and she knew it.

Lena figured that all of this must have been a result of what Marcus had done to Emma, but she couldn't understand why Emma would do the same cruel things to Celeste. Emma was definitely not the best friend Lena thought she was.

At one point Lena got up out of her chair and stood by the wall that was between herself and Celeste. With both hands pressed against the barrier she listened helplessly. Lena wasn't much on prayers, but she asked God to take over that night.

Meanwhile, back at Bubba's house the mood was real bad. His mother had cooked him a welcome home meal, but he didn't want it. The table was filled with all of his favorite foods. Her candied yams and greens were probably the best in the county. And nobody smothered pork chops like she did. Bubba held on to a piece of hot water cornbread so tight it crumbled on to the table and he didn't even notice. His mother watched with deep concern as he pushed his plate aside. She knew that of all the foods in the massive spread, his most favorite dish was her potato salad, and he didn't even put any on his plate.

"What's the matta', son? You sick to your stomach?"

"Yeah, Ma, somethin' like dat."

"I knew you shouldn't a-been tryin' to work so many days. You just a chile. Your daddy and me provide enough for you, don't we? Why you wanna go and do somthin' like that, huh? Workin' all them hours - all them days?"

Bubba slowly got up from the table and silently walked out of the room, leaving his worried mother to just stand and stare.

* * * * *

Big Mamma was partying and having a good time. She didn't show the slightest bit of concern. She was having a good night financially, and she didn't seem to mind in the least bit that her only child was sitting in a back bedroom waiting to be raped, for money.

One of the drunken men asked where Lena was. And after a moment they were all calling for her to come and sing, but there wasn't a song in Lena's heart that night. And when she said 'No' Big Mamma acted as if she didn't have a clue as to why She just laughed and told them that Lena must be on her period or something. And then they all laughed as the Cajun and country music blasted away on the hi fi player.

Lena looked out the kitchen window when she heard a noise, but she couldn't see anything. The back yard was pitch dark because there were no street lights out in the country. The men at the poker table didn't react to the sound, so she decided not to concern herself with it. That is, until she heard it again. This time the reflection of light from the kitchen window allowed her to spot a dark figure moving in the bush. Suddenly, all the anger that was building inside her was about to come to a head. If this was one of those ignorant ass-holes trying to sneak in the window to be first with Celeste, they were in for trouble. All of what Lena had only imagined doing was about to come to life as she picked up the biggest iron skillet she could find in the kitchen, and then headed out the back door.

At the same time Big Mamma had just opened Celeste's door. When she saw the terrified child in the corner, she revealed no shame. She went over to Celeste and pulled her up off the floor and proceeded to push her out of the darkened room, revealing a pretty young girl with a head full of 'platinum blond' hair. Big Mamma had dyed and curled Celeste's hair just like Esther Rose had done to her! Only Celeste was even more beautiful than Big Mamma ever was.

"No, Mamma, please don't do this!" Celeste begged. "Please don't make me go in there! I'm beggin' you! I want my grandma! Please - No-o-o!"

Big Mamma acted as if she couldn't hear the girl's cries. She just continued to push and drag Celeste to the nearby bathroom, and then said, "Wash your face so I can make you up again."

The bathroom was located across from Xavier's office, so he could hear Celeste more clearly as she begged and pleaded to be released. The cries were so painful that even Xavier had to stop working to listen. All the training in the world had not prepared him for this.

Lena held the skillet tight. She didn't know who was out there, but she did know that she was mad as hell, and was going to bash the first person that came around the corner of that house. Suddenly, she heard it again. Somebody was definitely in the bushes. She tipped quietly around the outside of the shrubbery, ready to pounce on whoever it was. Quietly she made it all the way up to the bush, and when the man's head slowly rose up out of the underbrush, she clanked him hard.

"Ouch!" cried Bubba.

"Boy, what you doin' out here this time'a night? I coulda' killed you!" Lena yelled.

"I wanna see Celeste." Bubba's heart was aching much more than the lump that was slowly rising up on his head.

Sympathy was written all over Lena's face. She would have never hit that boy if she had known who it was.

"I'm sorry, kid. But you shouldn't be here!"

She tried to imagine how bad he must have been feeling, but there was nothing either of them could do. It was a losing battle going up against Big Mamma, and Lena knew it. Even the law was inside Big Mamma's house that night.

"Go home, boy. There ain't nothin' you can do here."

"I'm goin' in there!"

"No, you ain't! They will kill you, son. This is a serious night. Ain't nobody gonna take your side in this matter."

Bubba changed from an over-grown angry young man to a heart-broken over-sized kid. He sat down in the dirt and started to cry. Lena didn't know what to do. She felt real sorry for him, but she knew that if he cried any louder, he would definitely be heard, and she didn't want that to happen, so she hugged him and tried to soothe his broken heart.

"Hush now. They'll hear you, son. I'm tellin' you, it's too late to help Celeste."

Ignoring everything that Lena said, teary-eyed Bubba suddenly lunged for Celeste's window, but he didn't quite make it. Bubba's weight did not allow him to jump but so high. His fingertips barely reached the windowsill, but he clung to it, determined to pull himself up and get inside. Lena grabbed hold of his pant leg and attempted to pull him back down, but she was such a little person that when she grabbed hold of him she was literally lifted off the ground as he struggled to get a better grip.

"Have you lost your mind, boy? I'm tellin' you to get down and go home!"

Suddenly one of the men came out of the back door to take a leak, and spotted Lena and Bubba struggling.

"Hey, what's goin' on out there?" The big ole lumberjack thought Bubba was trying to break into Celeste's room, so he lunged at Bubba, and missed. Lena knew the drunken fool was mistaking Bubba for an older person because of Bubba's size, and he would definitely hurt Bubba if he got hold of him, so she knew she'd better convince Bubba to go home.

"Get outta here, Bubba! You can't do nothin' but get hurt, son! These people will kill you!"

The man was just about to leap for the boy again when Bubba let go of the windowsill and reluctantly ran away. Lena played it off well. "That damned fool tried to get first dibbs on the girl. Can you believe that?" They both went back inside the house, arm in arm.

Big Mamma shoved Celeste into the bathroom and closed the door. Celeste just stood in there for a moment, wondering what was happening to her. She just could not understand why her mother wanted to do this to her. She had displayed nothing but love for Big Mamma from the day she arrived.

In the meantime, Xavier had stopped his calculator and sat quietly in his chair. He could not believe what he was hearing. He didn't know whether to go out in the hall and beg Big Mamma to let Celeste go, or to just go home and never come back again. No money in the world was worth witnessing this kind of torment, he thought to himself.

Celeste turned on the water faucet to wash her face, but she couldn't continue. She just stood there staring at the water pouring down the drain in the fancy imported porcelain sink.

Big Mamma was one of the first to have running water installed. And like everything else in the house, her bathroom was huge and fancy, with crystal knobs and velvet wallpaper, all decorated in red and black colors.

Celeste was just about ready to bend over and wash her face when she realized that somebody else was in the bathroom with her. Panic set in so hard that she froze. Somebody was behind the shower curtain, and she didn't know what to do. This time she knew that she wouldn't be able to muster up even an ounce of strength to fight back like she did in the park because she was all cried out. This time she was just a very frightened little girl with nobody to turn to. Her legs shook so hard her knees knocked together.

Celeste heard something fall in the bathtub that sounded like a small piece of metal. Her first thought was that the person had dropped the knife that he was about to kill her with. For a brief moment it felt comforting to know that somebody might just do away with her. She almost wished that it would be that simple because she had considered doing it herself.

Once again Celeste heard the piece of metal move around. It sounded like somebody was trying desperately to pick something up. Finally, she realized that whoever was behind the curtain was more focused on retrieving the metal object than on harming her, so she mustered up enough nerve to check it out. Holding her breath, she slowly peeked through the drape. And to her amazement, it was not the boogy man lurking in the tub, but Beatrice, one of Big Mamma's whores, crumpled up with a leather strap pulled tightly though its buckle around her upper arm. The woman was holding the other end of the strap with her teeth in order to get her collapsed and bruised vein to rise once more to receive her anxiously awaited injection of heroin. To Celeste's amazement, the metal sound she had heard was a hypodermic needle rolling around in the bath tub as if trying to escape the shaky hands of the desperate junkie. The woman hastily picked up the needle and stuck it in her arm and anxiously injected the drug into her vein. Celeste had never seen anything like that before. The deeply embedded track wounds in the woman's arm indicated that she must have been doing this for many years.

At first the woman didn't notice the young girl watching as she transformed from a crumpled and jerky drug addict to a calm and pseudo-sensuous whore.

"Hey, baby. You wanna try some-a dis?"

Celeste quickly closed the curtain and headed out the door only to be accosted by Big Mamma. This was a night from hell for sure.

"Let go of me!" Celeste screamed. "I'm not going to do this and you can't make me!"

And before Celeste knew it, Big Mamma had hit her so hard she saw black. Big Mamma had knocked her out.

At that moment Xavier swung open his door in an effort to assist the fallen young girl, but Big Mamma quickly put him in his place by shoving him forcefully back into his little office and slamming the door shut.

Celeste woke up a little later and didn't know where she was. But it didn't take long to find out that the nightmare was not over. Big Mamma had wiped off her face. Celeste was surrounded by nasty, liquor-smelling men. They were standing over her like hungry hogs in a trough.

"Damn, she's pretty," said one of the men.

When Lena heard the commotion she ran to see what was going on. She figured it had to have something to do with Celeste. And when she saw her goddaughter lying on the hallway floor, she didn't think about the fact that Big Mamma was close by and might hurt her if she interfered. She just pushed past everybody and knelt by Celeste. Big Mamma stood there for a moment and then walked away and went into the living room, leaving Lena to do whatever had to be done. Lena could have killed everybody in that house that night.

"Get out of here, all of you! Standin' over this child like she's a piece of meat! She's a child! A little girl! What's the matter with all'a you?"

Big Mamma heard Lena and rushed back into the hallway. By now Celeste had opened her eyes fully, but that didn't matter to Big Mamma. "What the fuck you think you doin', yellin' at my customers?"

Lena was out of control. "You know this ain't right, doin' this to your daughter! Look at her. She's just a baby!"

Lena held on to Celeste who was shaking badly. Big Mamma was instantly thrown into her evil mode. She bent down and stared at Lena in her usual despicable fashion. The veins in her neck were so big you could see them pulsating.

"Get outta my house," she said.

Lena just sat there and stared at Big Mamma. "You can't do this, Emma."

"I said get out!" Big Mamma pushed Lena away from Celeste and snatched the girl up from the floor and shoved her into the nearby bedroom. "And you, get in there!"

Lena begged, "Emma, please. Don't do this."

* * * * *

Xavier was totally devastated. He paced back and forth in the claustrophobic room. It was driving him crazy knowing that there was nothing he could do to help the frightened young girl. Not only would he have to literally fight Big Mamma, but he would also have to defend himself against all the men in that house. Finally, he sat down and put his head in his hands and wept. The situation was hopeless.

One of the more sober men came from the living room to check things out. He had on a deputy's uniform. "Everythin' alright?"

Big Mamma stared at Lena who remained upset, but said nothing.

"Is everything in order, Big Mamma?" He asked.

"Yeah, ain't nothin' goin' on out here."

"Where you want the Mayor to go?"

Big Mamma pointed to the same room she had just shoved Celeste into. When Lena saw that, she broke into tears. "Emma, you can't..."

And before she could get her words out the deputy led the old, fat, sour smelling Mayor into the room and closed the door behind them.

As soon as the two men entered, Celeste attempted to rush past them. But before she could reach the doorway the deputy caught her and held on to her as she kicked and screamed.

Outside in the hallway Lena and Big Mamma could hear Celeste screaming. Lena looked up at Emma with pleading tears in her eyes, but Big Mamma only stared back at her, daring Lena to move as she inhaled on her long Camel cigarette. Big Mamma flicked her ashes close to the edge of Lena's dress and walked out.

Celeste used her last bit of strength to fight off the big strong deputy, but it didn't work. He pinned her down on the bed while she kicked and screamed. The Mayor waited until all the fight was drained from her body, and then he moved closer.

"You're a strong little thing, ain't you? I like that." The Mayor proceeded to undress himself.

The deputy enjoyed holding Celeste down on the bed for the Mayor. But when the Mayor noticed that the more she squirmed, the more his deputy got aroused, he got mad. "Get outta here! I can take care of her now."

The deputy left, and Celeste just lay on the bed breathless.

When the deputy came out of the room Lena was standing there waiting. When he looked over at her, she spit in his face.

The deputy just looked at her, wiped his face and laughed, and then joined Big Mamma back in the living room.

The Mayor proceeded to take off his shirt and tie and pants. "Take that little ole' dress off, young'un, and let me see what you look like."

Celeste didn't move. She just stared at him in disgust. His baggy and colorful shorts looked ridiculous, but didn't compare to the disgusting belly that hung over them.

The deputy approached Big Mamma and asked, "What's wrong with Lena? She's sittin' outside that room like a junk yard dog protectin' its trash."

That statement did not sit well with Big Mamma. Was he calling her daughter trash? That was not a good thing. "Who you callin' trash?"

The deputy noticed the immediate change in Big Mamma's attitude. He had been on the wrong side of her before, and he didn't want to be there that night, so he clarified his statement. "Nobody, I just don't understand the problem. That girl in there could make more money tonight than I have ever seen in my whole life. All she gotta do is stop fightin' and act right."

Big Mamma was still not ready to let go of the 'trash' statement. She was like that. Once she focused on something, there was no letting go until she was satisfied. "But, who you callin' 'trash'?"

"I ain't callin' nobody trash. I just don't understand it that's all. I was just usin' the expression junk yard dog because they take so much pride in their - trash. You know what I mean?"

"I know what you better not mean! My daughter ain't no trash. She just don't understand how valuable she is, that's all."

"Her grandmother done put so much shit in her head about education and pride that she forgot to tell her about survival. I'm gonna show her how to survive," Emma bragged. "I'm gonna teach her that a body ain't nothin' but a body. And I'm just gonna show her how to use it, that's all. My daughter is gonna be rich!" Big Mamma yelled. "She's not gonna be runnin' around here lookin' like these other country bumpkins. She was born beautiful, and that's gonna be her ticket to a good life."

The deputy listened. Big Mamma was sincere. She didn't have a clue to what self-pride or dignity meant. She continued to explain things to the deputy that even she didn't understand. "Lena's just got a problem because she ain't never had no kids. She's got this idea that she ain't no good because she been in this business all her life. Shit, ain't nobody around here got nearly what we got, and I sure as hell ain't ashamed of it." Big Mamma walked through the crowd of lowlifes and started yelling to them all. "Hey, anybody here wanna be like me?"

Everybody yelled, "Yeah! Me! I do!"

Suddenly, one of the prostitutes jumped up from her chair and raised her drink and toasted Big Mamma. "To the best damned whore in the state of Louisiana!"

Everybody raised their glasses and whistled and yelled and

screamed their approval, but Big Mamma didn't. She liked the toast until the word "whore" was mentioned. This was the first time in all of her life that she had heard anyone refer to her as a whore. Nobody she associated with ever had the courage to call her names to her face. And Emma had isolated herself from those that might.

She blinked her eyes a little, and then left the room. Her blinking eyes usually came right before the veins popped out in her neck. And that always meant trouble for somebody. And since she didn't want to mess up this night she went to her room to calm down. Plus, she didn't quite know who she was mad at. She just knew that she felt a sudden deep-set ache in her heart when she was called a whore, and she couldn't rid herself of that pain.

* * * * *

As the Mayor got closer to Celeste, she backed up more. "Now, I told you to take your dress off, dahlin'. Don't make this difficult. It could be good for you and me. Here, let me help you." He reached for the strap on her dress, but she pulled back. "I guess you're still gonna be difficult." The 60-year-old man climbed up on the bed to get a better grip on Celeste, so she backed up even further. With her back against the headboard, she fought helplessly. Somehow he was able to clamp her two wrists in one of his fat hands and press them up against the wall behind the head of the bed. With the other hand he ripped off the top of her dress. The Mayor proceeded to grope at her exposed breasts, and lick as much of her bared body as he could while she squirmed and flinched. There was little Celeste could do because she was so completely exhausted.

Meanwhile, Bubba tossed and turned in his bed. There was no way he could sleep that night. He tried to imagine what might be happening to Celeste, but it was too painful. Each time he turned over he imagined those dirty old men pulling at her and possibly ripping off her clothes, but whenever he got to the thought of one of them in her, he would sit up and break out in a cold sweat. If he hadn't been raised well, he would surely have gone over there and blown every last one of those 'low-lifes' away.

Big Mamma stood in her room and looked at herself in the mirror, in the same manner she had when she first saw herself as a blonde. She wasn't quite sure of who she was seeing. Her entire life flashed before her as she remembered the childhood pain of Marcus's sexual penetrations, and all the self-serving foster homes, including Esther Rose and the man who raped her.

She remembered how the sneaky bastard would enter her room at night when his wife was asleep, and would put his big crusty hand over her mouth so that she wouldn't yell while he fondled and raped her night after night. She recalled how he threatened to turn her over to the juvenile authorities if she told. And most of all, she remembered how her foster mother accused her of causing him to do this, and then turned her over to the authorities anyway.

"What's this thing called 'life' about?" she thought.

Big Mamma placed her cigarette in a nearby ash tray and leaned closer to the mirror. The veins in her neck had begun to pulsate, as small beads of sweat popped out on her forehead and upper lip. Could this be the first time she looked at herself for what she had really become? Could there be a possible tear in her eye? Was she finally realizing that this was not the life she had intended for herself and her beautiful little girl? If it was, it only lasted a minute because after a brief moment of silence and self-doubt, she quickly wiped the sweat from her brow and lip, put on new bright red lipstick, picked up her cigarette and sauntered back into the living room. She changed up so fast she appeared to have two totally different personalities. But no matter how many personalities may have been hiding underneath that beautiful lemon colored skin, Big Mamma was the one running this house, and it looked like Big Mamma was there to stay.

Finally, the Mayor made one drastic mistake. He raised himself up a bit and then straddled his legs across Celeste in order to get a better grip on her dress so that he could pull it completely off. As he leaned over her, the smell of his sour whiskey breath was bad enough, but Celeste almost threw up when she felt his sweaty bloated stomach brush over her. The thought of this gross piece of blubber resting on her body was too much to bear. Celeste suddenly remembered her grandmother's words. "When their thinkin' ain't right, kick 'em in their pants." Well, he didn't have any pants on, but he was wearing those ridiculous shorts so... Celeste mustered up one more ounce of strength and 'wham!' she kneed him, right in his jewels!

The mayor let out such a scream that everybody in Big Mamma's house heard it. As a matter of fact, the entire county probably heard it. The intended rape was over, and the night ended early because the Mayor shut the place down for a week.

And as for Xavier, well, he took what monies he felt Big Mamma owed him and waited until nobody was around, and then slipped out the back door. He was finished with this house of ill repute and evil ways.

Chapter 11

Emma had never been to church before, so she was bound and determined to make this visit a good one. She felt that it was very important to choose the proper attire.

It was 10 o'clock on a Sunday morning. Emma stood solemnly in the open doorway of her bedroom closet staring at her massive wardrobe of brightly colored suits and tasteless dresses, all of which reeked of cheap perfumes and cigarette smoke. Tossed over the top of the closet door was her fluffy red boa. Emma slowly ran her fingers through the soft, luscious feathers and then reached for her black chiffon dress hanging nearby. She held it up in front of her. She danced and danced sadly around the room making the bottom of the dress twirl and swirl to the soft music of the Five Satins, "I Only Have Eyes for You." Emma was deeply troubled and the sensuous and mellow sounds of music seemed to help her disposition.

Nobody ever knew just how romantic Emma could be, but close friends did know how depressed she was capable of becoming. And on this day it looked as if she had finally hit the bottom. If someone had dug a deep hole in the middle of the floor of her bedroom that morning, she would have probably found it to be a saving grace because she would have most definitely climbed in it and vowed never to come out.

Emma liked the feel of soft feathers and flowing fabrics. It reminded her of movie stars and Hollywood, of Marilyn Monroe, Jane Mansfield and her favorite, Gypsy Rose Lee. As the music ended, she put the dress back on the rack and once again stood there looking for the perfect thing to wear, as her hi fi record player ejected the small 45 and proceeded to play another. This time it was Etta James' song, "All I Could Do Was Cry." The words from the song really touched Emma's heart as she stood there staring at a closet full of sexy clothes. All the things were there that she thought necessary to make a man happy. So, why couldn't she get one of her own? Tears came to her eyes as Etta James sang about 'losing the man that she loved, and all she could do was cry.' Emma could relate to this song so well. Why was she always alone? Why couldn't she find a man of her own? She just didn't have the answers so 'all she could do was cry.' And so she did. But it didn't stop her from searching her closet for the right dress to wear that morning. It was 10 o'clock on a Sunday morning. Emma stood solemnly in the open doorway of her bedroom closet staring at her massive wardrobe of brightly colored suits and tasteless dresses, all of which reeked of cheap perfumes and cigarette smoke. Tossed over the top of the closet door was her fluffy red boa. Emma slowly ran her fingers through the soft, luscious feathers and then reached for her black chiffon dress hanging nearby. She held it up in front of her. She danced and danced sadly around the room making the bottom of the dress twirl and swirl to the soft music of the Five Satins, "I Only Have Eyes for You." Emma was deeply troubled and the sensuous and mellow sounds of music seemed to help her disposition.

Nobody ever knew just how romantic Emma could be, but close friends did know how depressed she was capable of becoming. And on this day it looked as if she had finally hit the bottom. If someone had dug a deep hole in the middle of the floor of her bedroom that morning, she would have probably found it to be a saving grace because she would have most definitely climbed in it and vowed never to come out.

Emma liked the feel of soft feathers and flowing fabrics. It reminded her of movie stars and Hollywood, of Marilyn Monroe, Jane Mansfield and her favorite, Gypsy Rose Lee. As the music ended, she put the dress back on the rack and once again stood there looking for the perfect thing to wear, as her hi fi record player ejected the small 45 and proceeded to play another. This time it was Etta James' song, "All I Could Do Was Cry."

Big Mamma & Celeste

The words from the song really touched Emma's heart as she stood there staring at a closet full of sexy clothes. All the things were there that she thought necessary to make a man happy. So, why couldn't she get one of her own? Tears came to her eyes as Etta James sang about 'losing the man that she loved, and all she could do was cry.' Emma could relate to this song so well. Why was she always alone? Why couldn't she find a man of her own? She just didn't have the answers so 'all she could do was cry.' And so she did. But it didn't stop her from searching her closet for something to wear to church that morning.

Sometimes Emma would dress in costume and perform for higher paying clients. Her exotic outfits were very popular, but the most requested performance was that of a little girl. Emma had everything from knee-high socks and patent leather shoes to lace butt panties. Of course the crotch of the over-sized underwear was always missing. Emma was so child-like and precocious when she became that 'little girl' character that it was difficult to imagine this person being a hard-nosed businesswoman successfully dealing drugs and prostitution to the entire state of Louisiana. Yes, Big Mamma knew how to put on a show when the money was right. And all the time she was doing this, one would think that she was having the time of her life because she seemed to enjoy it as much as the men folk did. But when the show was over and the men were gone, and the sun came up, Emma always reverted back to the deeply troubled, angry woman that only her closest friends knew.

Emma chose to wear her red silk dress with the highest 'low-cut' neckline she could find in her closet. The dress was decorated in hand-sewn beads and imported lace. It was one of her most expensive garments. Emma felt good about her choice, but just couldn't figure out what to wear on her head. During one of her stays at a foster home, she was told that it is appropriate to cover your hair and arms when you enter a church, so she knew that she wasn't quite ready to walk out the door. What could she wear on her head, and what could she put over her arms? Instantly she reached for her favorite red boa, and since she had nothing to cover her head, she decided to pull her long black hair back in a tight conservative bun and stick a big red flower, that covered half her head, behind her ear.

After making sure that there were no runs in her stockings and the seams were straight, Big Mamma was satisfied. "This should do it," she thought to herself. Now, she was ready for Sunday morning service red spike heels and all

Emma sat in her car outside the church for a long time. She was having a few afterthoughts about this. "What goes on in one of these places?" she thought as she took one last puff on her cigarette. Emma had never been inside a church. What if somebody said something wrong to her? How would she react? If somebody's husband flirted with her, how would she handle that? Things were going through Emma's head so fast that she felt sick to her stomach. She put the cigarette out and was just about to start her car up and leave when she looked out her window and saw a sweet little gray-haired man in a long black robe with velvet trim standing on the front steps of the church waving at her. She tried to focus on his face to see if she knew him, but she didn't.

Emma could hear singing coming from inside the church. It

151

sounded good to her.

"Come on chile! Church is startin'! Hurry up now!" the little man insisted.

Emma didn't know what to do. She wanted to run away, but at the same time she wanted to go inside. Sweat started to bead up on her nose, and she thought to herself that if she didn't do something soon, she was going to mess up her good silk dress with perspiration. So she got out of the car and headed for the little ole assistant pastor.

"How you doin', Dahlin'?" He whispered. He was such a nice man. And he didn't seem to pay one bit of attention to Emma's big red outfit.

"I'm - just - fine, thank you." Emma was taken by the beauty of the stained glass windows inside the foyer. The sun was shining through the windows at just the right angle to make it look like what Emma imagined Heaven to be. "What a magnificent sight," she thought.

"I always stay outside for a few minutes after service starts because there are always folks tryin' to decide whether they comin' in or not, so I make their minds up for 'em." He grabbed Emma's arm and they proceeded to enter the church sanctuary.

The choir was singing and the congregation had just been seated, when Emma and her escort entered the church. The little man let go of Emma's arm and beckoned for her to find a seat anywhere she wanted. When one of the church ushers started to approach her, the little man waved him on. The wise old man may not have focused on Emma's clothes, but he was smart enough to know that she should be left to do her own thing. And by now Emma was so filled with awe that she forgot about all the people around her and was, in reality, doing her own thing. Right now all she was focusing on was finding a seat. And because she was so far in the back of the church, it was hard to do. Emma experienced a brief moment of fear and anxiety, so...

'Big Mamma,' appeared right on time - ready to take over and find a seat in that big ole church, and nobody was going to get in her way.

Confident that she looked good, Big Mamma gracefully sauntered down the aisle to the very front pew and proudly sat. By this time everybody had noticed her and started whispering. The women were furious that she was there, but the men were delighted. They couldn't believe that Big Mamma had actually come to church. Most of them had never seen her in the daytime except for the Louisiana Family Reunions. Even the preacher was pleasantly surprised at her presence as she sat and crossed her legs, adjusted her bodacious boa, and then winked at her favorite customer, the other Assistant Pastor, Rev. Elias P. Carter. This was the man Emma was so taken by. He was the one man she wished could be her own. He was the man Emma thought about whenever she listened to Etta James sing. Emma knew that he was the one person who could get her to give up her 'career.' If he had asked her to marry him, she wouldn't have hesitated to say 'yes.' But today she was about to find out that he was not the man she thought he was.

Church service went without incident. Because Emma was up front and focused on the preacher and his sermon, and was truly enjoying the service, she was oblivious to her surroundings. Big Mamma never looked back to see the disgruntled females, nor did she hear the snickering of the young people, or the gasps of the old. Her bright red outfit was definitely out of place, but she didn't have a clue. When the service was over, she walked out of church feeling great.

"Thank you for joinin' us, Miss Bouvier," said the Preacher as he shook Emma's hand. Emma smiled and responded with a bigger handshake. She still hadn't noticed the whispers behind her back because her first little escort was right back at her side making sure that she was satisfied with the service, and asking if she would consider coming back again. She promised him that she would return.

It felt so strange for Emma to be touched by men who weren't thinking about sex. The Pastor's gentle warm grip was so soothing she could have stood there holding on to him forever and a day. For once in her life Emma felt genuinely loved and almost respected.

"Is this what it feels like to have a real father or real brothers?" Emma wondered to herself. She checked the gray-haired preacher's soft brown eyes once more. "Could it truly be that this man saw her as a real person and not some cheap whore?" And then she answered her own question. Yes, sex was definitely not on his mind. Nor was that the intention of her attentive little escort.

"Oh, happy day!" Emma could have truly given both these men a great big hug and kiss on the cheek, but she knew better. She might have been oblivious to her surroundings at that time, but she wasn't a complete fool.

"No, Reverend, thank you!" Emma replied. "I needed that preachin' real bad." Emma felt so good inside. The sermon was about tithing and caring, so Emma put one hundred dollars in the plate.

"And thank you for your generous contribution, Sister. That was certainly more money than we've ever seen aroun' here." Emma smiled. "It's been long over-due, Sir."

"Well, we'll sure enough put it to good use. We thank you again, and may God bless you."

Emma left the warm and loving minister and the little old escort and headed for her car. She couldn't believe that they called her 'sister.' She had to look back several times to see if they were really standing there. They were there. And they even smiled and waved at her as she backed away, with her hand raised in 'goodbye.'

Emma felt so good inside she could have just jumped up in mid-air and screamed Hallelujah, even though she hadn't gotten a chance to speak to the other Assistant Pastor who had quickly vanished right after the service.

As she turned the key in her car door, Emma heard laughter nearby in the church parking lot. Two ladies were walking together and talking about her. They didn't see Emma standing by her car.

"Did you see that outfit?" one of the ladies blurted out.

"I never saw so much red in all my life," said the other one. "I thought that boa was goin' to get up and walk on its own it moved aroun' so much."

"Yeah, every time she flopped those feathers over her

shoulder they hit ole Lady Johnson in the face. You should'a seen that ole woman's expression."

"At least it stopped her from shoutin' so much. Miss Johnson gets on my last nerve sometimes. I don't know if the Lord really touches her that many times or if she's just tryin' to git touched by ole man Simpson."

"He do run to her and hold on to her every time, don't he?"

The two ladies laughed and walked on.

Emma was so hurt and angry. Nothing had prepared her for this moment. All that she wanted to do was to make peace with her Maker. And she thought that she had done just that until now. Anger was instantaneous. Big Mamma was back. For a brief second she considered getting in her car and running over everybody in her proximity. But instead she decided to do better than that. She was mad, and somebody was going to pay for it. And who better to do that than Assistant Pastor, Elias P. Carter?

"Where is that good-for-nothing-preacher?" she thought to herself. "Why did he disappear so fast after church? Was he ashamed of me? He's not going to get away with this!" So she headed angrily back across the church parking lot, big red boa and all. She knew that he was still there because she spotted his car behind the church.

The church pastor was still standing at the door shaking hands and talking to his parishioners when Emma went flying past him. The good Reverend had no idea where she was going. He and the remaining church members watched as Big Mamma looked under pews and turned over the collection table. The people were baffled. The Preacher was shocked. All they could do was stand there with their mouths open.

The high-blood-pressure veins protruded on Big Mamma's neck, and they weren't going to go down until she calmed down, and she wasn't about to do that until she found that chicken-shit preacher of hers.

Big Mamma burst open closet doors, looked in the men's rest room, and then headed for the minister's office, yelling "Elias Carter, I know you're in here somewhere!"

The women folk knew to stay out of Big Mamma's way, but one of the youth ministers wasn't afraid to approach her.

"Can I help you, Sister?" Obviously this young man was another person who had not visited her premises because she had never seen him before, and he didn't know who she was. And at this moment she really didn't care to hear the word,'sister' ever again in life.

"No, you cannot," she replied. "I'll find him wherever he is." She aggressively pushed the young man aside, almost knocking him over.

"But who are you lookin' for, ma'am?"

"That no-good-for-nothin' Reverend Carter! That's who I'm lookin' for, and I know I'm gonna find him around here some-place," she yelled.

"I think he's gone for the day, Miss..."

"Oh, yeah? Well, he sure did get outta here fast! And it sure is strange that he left his car in the parkin' lot!"

In the meantime, Big Mamma was still looking in and out of back rooms and behind office doors with the bewildered young man trying to assist the best way he could by opening the doors for her before she knocked them down.

Finally, Big Mamma hit pay dirt. Hiding behind one of the choir room doors, and sweating bullets, was the eminent, Rev. Elias P. Carter.

"What are you doin' hidin' back in there?"

"Oh, ah, I was just checkin' on somethin'."

"Checkin' on somethin'? Checking on something?" I'll check on somethin' for you!" Big Mamma instantly reached out, and before she knew it she had her hands around Elias' throat and she was choking the life out of him. And to his shock he could not break her grip. She was mad as hell, and she was determined not to let go of him until she finished beating him to a pulp.

The young man next to Emma was almost hysterical. He didn't know what to do. He started to run for help but didn't want to leave his church's assistant pastor to die. But he was scared to death to try and help the poor man. He wasn't about to go up against this mad woman. Not only was she almost a foot taller than he was, but she was definitely a foot wider.

"B-big, Ma-m-ma, take - your hands -off-my-neck!"

They struggled, but Elias couldn't win. Big Mamma kept holding on and squeezing his neck something fierce.

"Who do you think you are?" Emma yelled. "I'm good enough for you to come callin' at my place on Saturday nights, but I'm not good enough for you to speak to at your church?"

"I - don't -even know-you, lady!" Elias lied. He obviously said that for the sake of the people watching. But that was a big mistake. He didn't even think about the fact that he had just called her by her name. And Big Mamma knew it, and that made it worse. She choked him even harder. By now he was down on the floor and she was on top of him, choking him and banging his head all over the place.

The people watching saw Big Mamma grab the good reverend and begin to choke the life out of him, and they watched as he began to struggle for air, but it all happened so fast that nobody came to his aide. They probably could not believe that this woman was so strong. Finally, the pastor of the church burst through the group and attempted to remove Big Mamma's hands from around Elias's neck, but it didn't work. The old preacher just wasn't big enough or strong enough.

Big Mamma let go of Elias with one hand and gently pushed the little man aside with her other. It was so interesting to see that Emma made absolutely no attempt to harm the good Reverend. But, at the same time, her other hand was choking the mess out of Elias.

"Sister, please let go of Brother Elias," the preacher begged.

Big Mamma acted as if she never heard a word the preacher said. She was determined to beat Elias senseless. She had traumatized him so badly that the front of his pants suddenly became wet, and for a brief moment there was a splashing sound on the floor. Elias Carter had urinated on himself! The preacher jumped aside to keep from getting his robe wet. And Emma didn't care one bit that all those people were watching. She was so mad she probably didn't even realize that Elias had tinkled, until a little boy spoke up.

"Look, Mommy, Rev. Carter peed his pants!" The boy's mother put her hand over his mouth, and snatched him away from there, but then giggled to herself. She knew that this would be the talk of the town on Monday. And she couldn't wait to get it started on Sunday. And she planned to start with Elias's brand new wife who, by the Good Lord's Graces, hadn't come to church that day.

Big Mamma finally let go and dropped Elias flat. He lay there wet and smelly, and gasping for air. She felt that she had truly gotten her revenge as she adjusted her boa, picked up her red flower off the floor, pushed through the nosy on-lookers, and walked out of the church with her head held high. But in reality, Emma was devastated.

Chapter 12

Walter Lee, Bubba and Cleotus were down by the river digging worms out of the mud so that they could go fishing. It turned out that the boys really did have a favorite spot for worms. The fat and slimy creatures were all over the place, and the boys were in this mud up to their ankles. How could they stand it? Worms were everywhere, and they didn't even have shoes on. Of course T-Bone was standing on the side watching. He was adamant about not allowing his raggedy, but spotless, old tennis shoes with overly stretched dress socks get anywhere near that mud hole. Besides that he wasn't about to stab a defenseless little worm with a deadly hook just for the sake of fishing. He just wasn't going to do it.

Each of the other boys had his own tin can, and was systematically pulling the worms out of the ground. Sometimes it looked like a real tug-of-war. The boys pulled on the six-inch long worms, and the worms pulled back. Some got away and some didn't. The boys knew how to have fun. While doing this, they sang, danced and teased each other. What a life! Walter Lee loved being with his friends and digging for worms. "I got another one! Damn, I love this. Look at this one! Shit, we gonna catch some fish today!"

Walter Lee plopped his final worm in his can and proceeded to pick up his home-made fishing pole, burlap sack and brown paper lunch bag and head for their favorite fishing hole. The other boys followed. However, Bubba grabbed his gear and lagged a little behind the others. He had been feeling pretty low lately. Walter Lee decided to try and pull Bubba out of his bad mood. "Bubba, you gotta get it together, man. You wouldn't want that girl now, anyway. Not after all them men been with her."

"I know. Ain't nothin' wrong with me." Bubba was lying like a champ and Walter Lee knew it. "I know you ain't tryin' to convince me because you been lookin' like a whipped dog for a month now."

This annoyed Bubba. "Get off my nerves, Walter Lee. I don't want to hear nothin' from nobody, you hear?"

"Yeah, I hear." Walter Lee knew when to leave Bubba alone. Now!

Cleotus was the only one doing just fine. "All ya'll shoulda' kept your shit in your pants like I did and none of ya'll would be freakin' like you are. My daddy say you don't have to have sex if you ain't ready just cause somebody else wants you to."

Bubba did not want to hear anything from anybody right now. "Shut up, Cleotus! I still owe you one for runnin' out on us. I ain't forgot it neither."

T-Bone tried once again to keep peace. "I don't think now is the time to mess with Bubba, Clee."

Cleotus defended himself. "Why is everybody pickin' on me? I ain't done nothin' but save myself some unnecessary grief, that's all."

Bubba was still mad at him. "Well, you ain't seen no grief 'til I commence to whippin' on your head. And from now on, I want you to call me by my proper name."

Cleotus still didn't quit. "You been 'Bubba' since you was born."

Bubba was really mad now. He knew Cleotus was still messing with him. "My name is John Edward Bradley and don't you forget it! I done outgrew 'Bubba.' I don't like it no more except from special friends, and you ain't one of 'em."

For some reason Cleotus was really in a brave mood. He continued to harass Bubba. "Okay, John Edward, but how you gonna remember it? I recall the teacher sayin' that you'd lose your nose if it wasn't attached to your face."

Well, that did it. Bubba moved up on Cleotus fast. He

reached for him, but Clee was too quick. Once again the squirrel was moving fast in order to get away from Bubba's clutches. Cleotus and his fishing pole were suddenly behind T-Bone. Bubba would get so mad when Cleotus moved fast like that.

"Boy, one of those days..." Bubba threatened. He was so mad he couldn't complete his sentence.

T-Bone, holding his fishing pole and a very clean pail, pushed Cleotus back in front of him. He liked being in the back following the other boys. This way he could take more time to look at the ground and make sure not to step in mud holes that might mess up his shoes. Cleotus made sure not to get too close to Bubba who was so mad that he was no longer walking slowly.

The boys, all but Bubba, walked along the riverbank having a good time. One would assume that they could hear music because they walked, jumped and sometimes danced in step with one another. Cleotus was so talented, he should have been on television. The boys could even sing acappella. Their music was magical. Bubba listened to them sing while he loaded his hook with one of the worms. Beyond Bubba was Walter Lee, casting his makeshift rod into the water. To the other side of Walter Lee was Willie T-Bone, baiting his hook with something from his pail. Nobody ever knew what T-Bone used because he wouldn't tell, but you can be sure it wasn't anything that squirmed. The other boys always laughed at T-Bone, but he didn't care.

"Why ya'll wanna stick those poor worms with that hook, I'll never understand."

Walter Lee found that comment ridiculous. "How some-body from down here in the country can be so scared of worms, I'll never know."

Walter Lee went out on the rocks. He was trying to be real careful because the river was pretty rough that day. The other boys spread out. Everybody went to his own special spot. Walter Lee fought the current in the water. "The river is high today, ya'll."

"It rained last night, dummy. And you don't need to be way out there on them rocks. One slip and you're gone and we can't help you." T-Bone lectured.

Walter Lee would not be himself if he didn't show off about something. "You don't know who you talkin' to. I been fishin' on these rocks all my life."

Bubba finally joined in the conversation. "Best fishin' is after the rain."

T-Bone was really concerned about their safety. "I know, but that river is movin' fast."

Bubba cast his pole out across the water. "Yeah, it's pretty rough. But we should be able to catch somethin'."

There was a moment of silence as all the boys cast out their lines. The cheerful chirping of the birds and the warm summer breeze cast an aura of peace over the riverbank. This gave Bubba time to do exactly what he had been trying not to do for a whole month, think. He moved closer to the rocks in order to talk to Walter Lee. He wanted to ask Walter Lee something, but didn't know how to approach the question. He had been trying to get up enough nerve to do this for a long time. "Walter Lee?"

"Yeah?"

"You been back to Big Mamma's, ain't you?"

"Yeah."

Walter Lee threw his line out. Bubba waited a moment before asking more questions. "Um, have you... Have you been with..."

"I can't hear you, Bubba." Walter Lee pulled his line in and threw it out again.

Bubba tried to get closer, but the rushing river intimidated him, so he stopped and tried to speak louder. "Have you - been with..."

Bubba couldn't bear the thought of Walter Lee saying that he had been with Celeste, so he changed the question. "Have you - seen - Celeste?"

"No."

Bubba wasn't sure if Walter Lee was saying this to make him feel better or not, but it worked. But Bubba still needed more information. "What do you mean, you ain't seen her? You had to see her if you been there."

"Yeah, I been there, but I ain't seen Celeste."

"Well, who come out the door to get you?" Bubba was confused.

"Nobody."

Walter Lee just wasn't giving Bubba enough information. This frustrated Bubba. "What do you mean, nobody?"

"I mean what I say. Nobody. Big Mamma just been yellin' out the window."

Bubba was really curious now. Celeste must be taking so many men now that she couldn't even help Big Mamma. "Well, where was Celeste? She - yellin? - out the window - too?"

"No. I ain't seen her or heard her. I suppose she's there, though."

"Why?"

"I don't know. I just suppose so. Where else would she be?"

Walter Lee wanted to stop talking and fish. Bubba tried to think of something, but couldn't figure out the answer. "I don't know."

They both continued fishing - quietly - when suddenly there was a loud splash in the water. Cleotus had had some luck with the fish. "I got one!"

The boys looked over to see that Cleotus had caught a winner.

"Boy, look here what I got!" Cleotus yelled.

A big fish fought Cleotus to get free. Cleotus's fishing pole was bent just about as far as it could. "I don't think I can hold this one!"

The boys saw that Cleotus had caught a big fish. He was struggling hard.

Walter Lee yelled from out on the rocks. "Damn, he's got a good one. Don't let it get away, Clee!"

Cleotus struggled. "Somebody better get over here and help me with this sucker!"

Walter Lee almost dropped his pole into the river watching Cleotus.

"You can handle it, Clee," he yelled. "Just work with it!"

Cleotus's feet slipped deeper and deeper into the muddy bank of the river. He got really nervous. "No, I think I'm gonna let it go!"

Bubba decided to go and help him. Bubba stuck his pole down in the mud in case he got a nibble. But as soon as he walked away from his pole, the pole started to slip so he returned to readjust it. T-Bone saw the size of the fish.

"Man, that's big! Hold on to it, Clee! Don't let go!" T-Bone yelled.

Cleotus's feet slipped more. He got closer and closer to the river's edge. He was about to slip into the river. "Oh boy, I think I need help ya'll. I'm slippin'!"

The boys realized that he really was slipping into the water. Bubba had readjusted his pole and was on his way to help his screaming little buddy. "I'm comin', Clee!" Bubba yelled as he moved faster.

"I can't hold on to it no more!" Cleotus pleaded. His feet were no longer visible. "I'm slippin, ya'll!"

He let go of the fishing pole, which quickly vanished into the racing waters. And it was beginning to look as if Cleotus was going to be right behind the pole because by now he was almost up to his waist in mud at the edge of the river. He was going in! Walter Lee stared in disbelief from the rocks. He was frozen.

"Cleotus, No!"

Bubba got to Cleotus just in time to grab his shirt, but now Bubba was sinking, and because he was heavier than Cleotus, he went down faster and right behind Cleotus. Walter Lee was trying his best to get off the rocks, but couldn't move fast enough. He dropped his pole into the river. Willie T-Bone was racing toward them. He lost one of his shoes in the mud and finally ran out of his other one. He arrived in time to hold on to Bubba before Bubba went under, but it was a struggle because Bubba was so much heavier than T-Bone. By now Cleotus was definitely in the river and holding on to Bubba with all his might. Walter Lee raced to their aid. "Hold 'em, Bubba! I'm comin'! Don't let 'em go!"

Walter Lee almost slipped into the river, but kept on going. He hadn't even thought about the danger he was in. He moved like he could walk on water if he had to in order to save his friend.

Cleotus was almost pulling Bubba in because of the force of the river. T-Bone was looking for something to hold on to because Bubba was too heavy for him, and Bubba was trying to hold on to Cleotus.

Cleotus had the most desperate look on his face when he finally cried out pitifully... "I can't - swim!"

Bubba was horrified. Nobody knew that Clee couldn't swim. T-Bone was now holding on to Bubba's coverall pocket and strap. The pocket ripped off, and now all T-Bone had was Bubba's strap, and Bubba was stuck too far in the mud to back up. Walter Lee struggled to get there, but he just couldn't seem to move fast enough. "I'm comin, ya'll! I'm comin'!"

T-Bone's hands were bleeding from the buckle on Bubba's strap. He cried, "Oh, my God!"

Walter Lee arrived and reached for T-Bone when suddenly

Bubba's fingers couldn't hold Cleotus anymore. Cleotus was washed away. The boys couldn't take it. Bubba was horrified. "Oh, Jesus - No!"

T-Bone was in shock, but still didn't let go of Bubba. "No, God - No!"

Walter Lee let go of T-Bone and raced down along the river's edge. "We got to get him! I'm gonna get him!"

The frail little body washed away, with Cleotus's arms flailing in desperation. Bubba started to go into the river after him, but T-Bone stopped him. "No, you can't go in there! We'll get 'em."

T-Bone struggled to get Bubba out of the mud. Walter Lee was long-gone.

"Cut 'im off, Walter Lee! Cut 'im off!" T-Bone yelled and pointed to a floating log.

Walter Lee, jumped on to the log and made it out to the center of the moving water just as Cleotus went by. He reached out to grab Cleotus, but it was too late. Walter Lee was devastated. He ran back from the log and on to the riverbank. By now the other boys had passed him and were headed down the river after Cleotus. Everybody had gotten their minds together. They just concentrated on saving their helpless little buddy who had gone under several times. They thought, "Thank God the moving river kept bringing him to the surface." Walter Lee ran so fast that he looked like a beautiful stallion racing through the woods.

Suddenly the boys came up against another obstacle. Down the river they could see dozens of rocks protruding out of the water. They knew that if they didn't get to Cleotus by the time he got to those rocks, it would definitely be too late.

Bubba, while running and trying desperately not to lose sight of Cleotus, spotted a long pole. He lifted the pole as if it only weighed 5 lbs. and then yelled back at T-Bone who was following close behind him.

"Grab it! Grab it!"

T-Bone didn't know what Bubba wanted him to do with it, but he grabbed it anyway. They were both still running a little ahead of Cleotus's body. Finally Bubba found the right time to toss his end of the pole far into the water ahead of Cleotus. Bubba figured that Cleotus would see the pole and would grab it. And even though it was damn near impossible for T-Bone to maintain a grip on this stick that was almost as big as he was, he somehow kept a hold on it until Bubba was able to assist him. Bubba yelled, "Hold on to your end. Don't let go! Hold it, T-Bone!"

Bubba ran back to T-Bone, and at the same time, yelled to Cleotus as his limp little body approached the pole. Bubba and T-Bone held on tight, hoping that Cleotus would grab it. They both yelled and screamed.

"Grab it, Clee! Grab the pole! Take the pole!!"

"He can't hear us!" T-Bone was devastated. He yelled at Cleotus again. "Cleotus! Take the pole!"

Bubba cried uncontrollably. "Grab it, Clee! Please grab it."

Walter Lee was far ahead of them. He was almost at the rocks. At first he was horrified when he saw a 100 foot drop nearby, but knew that he had to climb out there, if he planned to save Cleotus.

Bubba and T-Bone were still trying to make Cleotus grab the

pole. As Cleotus approached the pole, the boys thought they had him. The pole was practically touching the body. Finally, it did touch him, catching a piece of his clothes. Bubba screamed to Cleotus. "Grab it, grab it, grab it!"

T-Bone begged Cleotus too, with all his heart. "Take it, take it, take it!"

Bubba cried harder because it appeared that Cleotus was not conscious. Bubba and T-Bone were exhausted. T-Bone was almost in shock but he continued holding on because he knew that this was his last chance. The pole ripped Cleotus's shirt as he washed past it. The boys were speechless.

Walter Lee was the last hope, and he knew it. He was determined not to let this body get past him. He saw that the river was washing Cleotus to the left, so he worked his way to the left when suddenly Cleotus was flipped to the right so he worked his way back to the right. Walter Lee was soaking wet and tired, but his determination to see this through was awesome. And even though he was a small guy, the determination in his eyes lent hope to the situation.

Finally, the body arrived, limp and flowing whichever way the water took it. With arms outstretched, Walter Lee dove on to the body and held on to it. He got Cleotus by the neck and was trying desperately to get a good hold on the rest of him while he braced himself against the slippery rocks. By now Bubba and T-Bone were quickly approaching. They saw Walter Lee and Cleotus in the water and raced to help. They struggled over the rocks, aware at all times of the nearby waterfall, but not caring. Finally they reached Walter Lee and the limp body of Cleotus. But, how would they get off the rocks? They all sat holding on to Cleotus and looking back over the rushing river. Walter Lee was the most exhausted. Bubba flipped Cleotus over on the rocks to try and revive him. He held Cleotus as T-Bone tried mouth to mouth resuscitation. Walter Lee was too exhausted to assist. He just watched with hopefulness, but it was too late. Cleotus Murphy was dead. The boys didn't want to accept this. They continued crying and trying. T-Bone begged Cleotus... "Ah, com'on, Clee. Com'on, man."

Bubba was still determined to do something. "Try it again, dammit!"

T-Bone tried again. Walter Lee regained his strength. "Let's get him off the rocks!"

"How?" T-Bone was exhausted.

"Like this!" Bubba flung Cleotus over his back and proceeded to walk the rocks. The other two boys assisted as best they could in holding Bubba up.

When they finally got to the riverbank and laid Cleotus on his back, it was obvious that he was dead. T-Bone looked at the other boys. He and Bubba had finally accepted Cleotus's death. But Walter Lee couldn't. "I'm gonna get help!" He took off running.

Bubba yelled after him. "Walter L-e-e! It's too late!"

Walter Lee didn't want to hear it. He was filled with emotion as he ran and ran and ran and ran, crying.

Chapter 13

1998 - The sun was shining bright over the flat New Mexico Highway. Racing east at a high rate of speed was a new Black BMW Coupe. The tinted windows were rolled up tight to keep the scorching heat from filtering in on the sweet smelling black leather seats. The car moved fast and smooth past fields of cattle, rest areas, and any truck, trailer or car that was going less than 80 miles per hour. As it approached slower traffic, the car worked its way in and out of the lines of vehicles until it came to a place where it had no choice but to slow down.

Frustration and anxiety caused a flashback in time to race through the driver's mind...

An unkempt Caucasian man's hand reached out and attempted to squeeze the large firm breast of a young and healthy Black teenage girl. Through the bright red flowered sundress, the little girl's golden brown skin heaved with disdain as she angrily smacked the man's grubby hands away.

The expensive black leather gloves shifted downward from 5th gear to 4th. The car was quickly closing in on a fully loaded Mack truck already in the passing lane. The truck was attempting to pass another overloaded, and even slower, big rig. The BMW couldn't get around the two massive vehicles, so it shifted down again. Slower traffic was in front as well as in back of the impatient automobile.

The driver continued to remember...

The chalky hands reached out once again for the young girl, pulling at the top of her dress and bra, partially exposing a beautiful and healthy breast and shoulder. The girl jumped away as...

The Mack truck finally passed the other rig and got back into the slow lane. The road was once again open to the driver who was now back on target. Old memories ceased momentarily as the expensive black boot pushed the clutch to the floor and quickly shifted back up to 4th gear, passing the gigantic vehicle, and then back up to 5th, and once again off and speeding down the endless superhighway. Once again allowing the driver to think...

The young girl's dress flew high above her knees, exposing her large firm thighs and her white cotton panties as she scooted across the floor trying to get away from the man's groping fingers. The struggle was intense. The breathless cries of the young girl revealed just how determined she was to stop this man from touching her. She fought hard. Finally, the man got his hands on her panties and was about to pull them off when suddenly the determined little girl kicked with all her might, and landed a swift hit right in his JEWELS! Needless to say, he screamed at the top of his lungs...

The driver reminisced no more. This prince-of-a-car was off and flying once again. The expensive wheels of the somewhat dusty beemer were once again breaking all speed limits. On the front seat of the car lay a beautifully decorated invitation 'Let's Re-unite Our Louisiana Families', and written on the front of the envelope was a poorly handwritten note which simply said, "Please come."

The crimson sunset could barely be seen as the sun went down behind the tall buildings of the city of Shreveport, Louisiana. The eerie evening light caused the big skyscrapers to take on the appearance of exaggerated monstrous shadows waiting to pounce on the evening traffic, while this anonymous black maverick escaped across the local freeway, headed for the rural countryside.

The night was hot, humid and foggy. Raindrops fell rhythmically from the leaves of the Louisiana pine trees and landed heavily on the muddy ground below. A Black man, in his fifties, wandered aimlessly along the flooded riverbank. Occasionally, the weary and dirty man turned a bottle of cheap wine up to his quivering lips and swallowed it anxiously. Distraught, he started pacing back and forth as he watched the raging waters rush by. The troubled man seemed to be anticipating someone or something soon to come down the muddy river. He sat and stared and waited. And finally, it was there! He became excited and quickly sat on the ground and proceeded to untie his shoelaces and remove his old, worn-out shoes. It was obvious by the condition of his hard and brittle feet that he had not worn socks for some time. Once He got up to see if what he had spotted was still there. And it was! Something dark and oddly shaped was floating downstream, and this man was determined to retrieve it. The object headed for the river's edge. The man got as close to the river as possible, trying to reach the floating mass, but his feet started to sink deeply into the mud. It appeared that if he moved one inch closer to the edge, the rushing river would swallow him up. And suddenly it did just that! His feet were so deep in the mud that when the water got above his ankles it seemed like it just grabbed hold of his legs and sucked him in like quicksand!

Kicking up mud and gravel, the black BMW finally arrived, racing alongside the deadly riverbank with the same amount of force and speed as if it was still on the local highway. The car seemed to ignore all bumps, ditches and rocks on the dark back road, and continued on as fast as lightening, never noticing the drowning man over the embankment in the nearby river.

Suddenly, with the same amount of force as the racing maverick, the drowning man's head popped up out of the water desperate for air. Having been washed downstream where the waters were calm, he was able to stay afloat and make it to the river's edge. He lay there a moment gasping for air, and then finally rolled over on his back to rest as confusion consumed his mind.

The black BMW Coupe racing across the countryside finally reached its destination. The mysterious beemer's speeding tires raced alongside the river.

The troubled unknown man was lying down with his head propped up on a tree trunk by the riverbank, asleep. His bare feet were deep in the mud and his clothes were soaked from the previous night when he had fallen in the river and almost drowned. The raging waters rose higher and higher as each ripple quickly disappeared downstream.

Kicking up dust and gravel, the speeding tires of the beemer made enough noise racing down the old road to startle the sleeping man below the embankment. It was still not clear who he was, but it was clear that he was disappointed with the arrival of the morning sun which forced him to go through another day of watching and waiting at the river's edge. He knew that the only thing that could make him feel better right then would be the sweet taste of cheap wine, so he proceeded to look for the bottle he had had the night before. Finally, he found the precious brown paper bag that held the only thing that got him through each day. He put it to his chest and held on to it as if it were made of gold.

Big Mamma's house stood alone across the distant field. The old frame structure looked different now. Surprisingly, there were no cars parked in the yard, and the old wooden bench that sat outside the house for the teenage boys was gone. Serenity seemed to have engulfed the entire half-acre of property. The phantom car approached Big Mamma's house and slowed down and then slowly pulled into the driveway. The car sat a moment and then drove off quickly.

Immersed in thought, the tattered man by the river turned his bottle of wine up to his mouth. It was empty. He licked the rim hoping for one last taste, but it was all gone. He tossed the bottle up in the air, and when it landed it shattered inside the brown paper bag.

On the other side of the county a banner, once again, stretched across the main entrance of the park. It read: WEL-COME - REUNITED LOUISIANA FAMILIES '98. The music was live! It was the latest sound - from Blues to Rap to R&B to Reggae, and the crowd was enjoying it. No longer was the dance platform made of old wood, nor were the children quite as ragged as in the fifties, but the family spirit had not changed. People of all races came once again. The food smelled good and the tent with the watered-down beer, still had the longest line.

The strong nasal tone of a Southern White man's twang vibrated over the sound of the music and the noise of the crowd.

"Welcome, everybody! This is our first reunion in 40 years, and we are happy seein' ya'll here. God Bless you! Have a good time!"

Everybody applauded and began to party hard. The live band was excellent. The only difference in the music was that the musicians played hip-hop rather than honky tonk. The local band was right on time with the beat, and the singers were jammin'. The disc jockey had his act together too. This family reunion was really happening!

On one side of the platform sat a cute little old woman in her seventies obviously being pursued by a handsome elderly man in a suit and bow tie. It was an interesting scene because even though the couple was of considerable age, they both stood out amongst the crowd. The little lady was dressed a bit too youthful, one might say, but she looked good in her bright colors and white high heel shoes. Throughout the dancing and singing, the couple was completely engrossed in their private conversation. Several times the man with the bow tie had to put his mouth close to her ear so that she could hear what he was saying because the music was so loud. But she didn't seem to mind. It was obvious that she liked him.

The couple was sitting in seats that had been placed close to the stage for a reason. And that reason was because this little ole lady was Lena, Big Mamma's old-time friend. She was still an important part of this backwoods county, and obviously still able to attract the attention of some men folk.

The program was about to begin. The announcer tried to get everybody's attention as he introduced the now, grown-up, Willie 'T-Bone' Hightower.

"Folks, listen up! Listen up! Back to celebrate our ole-time reunion, right from these very backwoods of Louisiana himself, we welcome the Reverend Willie T. Hightower. One of the most respected ministers in the country and a prime candidate for the US Ambassadorship to South Africa."

The crowd roared with excitement. They applauded and applauded. The women and young girls were in awe of this handsome preacher. He looked so successful with his tailor made clothes 'that fit' and his imported Italian shoes. Looking at this man, one would surely forget about the old hand-me-down worn- out tennis shoes and skinny legs sticking up out of those baggy black dress socks. Yes, indeed, T-Bone had reached his goal in life.

Back on the dusty country road the BMW was still rushing to get to its seemingly endless destination. Inside the car the Giorgio Armani sunglasses checked the speedometer which indicated 80 miles per hour. The glasses also looked through the rear-view mirror for the law. Nobody was following.

On the platform Willie T. took the microphone and attempted to speak, but the crowd was so proud of him that they continued applauding and yelling. Finally he quieted them down. "Ladies and Gentlemen, and all you young folks out there - it is truly an honor for me to come home to such a warm welcome. I can't begin to tell you how much all this means to me."

The people applauded again, but Willie T. quieted them down with his raised hands. "This place has so many good memories for me, and some sad ones too, but we learn to go on. So, thanks for coming out, and have a good time! God bless you all!" The people really loved him.

The BMW finally reached its destination. As it pulled into the parking lot on the county grounds, the music and noise completely drowned out the already quiet engine. The black beemer quickly and silently slipped in and out of the rows of cars, eagerly seeking out any open space that would allow this dusty, bug-spattered phantom to rest. The announcer took the microphone from Willie T.

"And now folks, our special treat. We have for you today, the one and only person responsible for this reunion. She is the one person we all know and love. We used to call her Big Mamma, but we only know her today as Mamma Bouvier."

The people applauded and whistled. Big Mamma was now 76 years old and ill. Her weight had greatly diminished. She walked slightly bent over with a cane, but her Creole beauty was still holding. The announcer and Willie T. helped her to the microphone.

Far in the back of the parking lot the BMW squeezed into a space. The driver's car door opened and the black snakeskin boots stepped out, accented by well-tailored black gabardine slacks. The driver rushed so quickly toward the dance platform in a large hat, oversized black trench coat and big sunglasses that it was almost impossible to recognize who it was.

Big Mamma stood at the microphone while the people applauded her. She finally spoke to them. "How is everybody?"

The people yelled and whistled and waved to her. Willie T. stepped up and helped her with the microphone. He placed it closer to her mouth. Like the rest of her body, her voice was weak.

"Lord knows I've done a lot of things in my life that I'm not too proud of, but puttin' on these reunions never was one of them."

The people applauded more. Mamma Bouvier waited for applauds to stop, and then she spoke again. "Some of you don't remember those times, but those of you who do, know what I mean."

Mamma Bouvier repositioned her feet, as Willie T. remained close by. Her meek and gentle smile left her face as she continued. "These reunions were to keep the families of this here county carin' for each other. But what I didn't realize was - while I was tryin' to bring everybody together, I was also tearing families apart with my misdoin."

She tried to stand up straight and tell it like it really was. "Yes, I was the one who paid for the Louisiana Reunions." Everybody clapped again, but she made them quiet down by waving her hand. "No, listen to me. I thought that if I put some of the money that I made from the men folk in this here county back into somethin' positive every year, it would make up for my misdoin, but I was wrong. I hurt a lot of people..."

Mamma Bouvier became a bit emotional. Her lip began to tremble and her legs got a little weak. The cane she depended on so heavily started to shake, but Willie T. was there to hold her up. He gently placed his hand on top of her hand and steadied the cane by gently pressing down. She was okay now.

An old White man yelled from the crowd. "You helped a few of us too, you know?"

Some of the people laughed. Mamma Bouvier smiled out of

appreciation of his support, but she didn't find it funny because she was here to apologize for those very actions.

"Well, but - no, it wasn't right for me to do those things and I'm here today to say, I'm sorry." A woman in the crowd yelled out to her. "We forgive you, Mamma Bouvier."

The people agreed. Lena had tears in her eyes. Mamma Bouvier was full inside. "Thank you. Thank you all."

As the people applauded again, the mystery person pushed through the crowd, trying to get to the platform, but it was difficult. Everybody thought that Mamma Bouvier's speech was over and she looked like she was about to walk away, but something was bothering her. She took the microphone back. Willie T. got their attention again.

"Hold it, wait just a minute, folks."

The band struck a loud musical chord in order to get their attention. She spoke again.

"Some of ya'll remember I had a daughter. She was very special to me, but I ran her away with my selfishness, and I ain't seen her in almost forty years. I had hoped this reunion would bring her back to me."

Pushing through the crowd, the mystery person's sunglasses were knocked to the ground, but the person didn't try to pick them up because the person was too busy rushing and pushing people aside to get to the platform. Mamma Bouvier continued...

"I had hoped that maybe God could forgive me just this once and let me see her again before I leave this earth - because I'm not well."

The crowd moaned at the bad news.

"But I guess He ain't quite ready yet." Her voice broke. "Anyway, - I know ya'll been blessed - so have a good time on me. Thank you." She was finished.

Mostly everybody was in support of Mamma Bouvier. Some had tears in their eyes. Some just applauded. Some whistled. In the meantime, this mystery person's hat flew off and of course revealed Celeste. She jumped up on the platform, and for the first time in 39 years Celeste was face to face with the woman who tried to sell her to a bunch of drunken rapists. For the first time in 39 years she had the opportunity to look in this woman's eyes and ask her, "Why?" But Celeste didn't do that. Once she was face to face with Mamma Bouvier she knew that there was no room in her heart for hatred. The years she spent in professional counseling helped her to better relate to the outside world. The years she spent studying the word of the bible from her church pastor taught her forgiveness, and her grandmother's death, when she was 21 years old, taught her the value of life.

Celeste grabbed Mamma Bouvier, who was staring at her with a combination of shock and shame. With tear-filled eyes, Mamma Bouvier finally relaxed, and warmly received the most wanted and needed hug she could have ever imagined. The two women cried uncontrollably as they carefully examined each other, at which time the crowd went wild with cheers of support.

Celeste was more gorgeous than ever. A little Chinese man in his fifties yelled with delight. "Look! That's Big Mamma's daughter, Celeste!"

His wife looked at him with an evil eye. "How do you know it's her daughter?" Well, the guilt was written all over the man's face. He gave a stupid look and shrugged his shoulders. "I don't know nothing!"

It was clear that he was the little Chinese boy who had brought Big Mamma Cokes for an extra five minutes. He gave his wife a stupid laugh as she stared coldly at him. So, he tried to make it better. "You want a Coca Cola?"

Celeste walked slowly alongside Mamma Bouvier, holding on lovingly in an attempt to help her down off the platform. Willie T. was on the other side of the ailing old woman.

"You sure turned out to be a real beauty, Celeste." Willie T. said.

"Thank you, Willie T."

Mamma Bouvier agreed. "He's right. You are beautiful, daughter."

Celeste smiled and hugged Mamma Bouvier and thanked her as well.

Willie T. grabbed them both and started walking. "Actually, I've got the two most beautiful women in this here county on my arm today."

Celeste, Mamma Bouvier and Willie T. strolled along, holding on to each other. And then Celeste remembered Lena.

"Hey, where is Auntie Lena? She's not..."

"Dead?" Mamma Bouvier said.

Celeste nodded, yes.

"No. She's out there somewhere still tryin' to catch herself a man. She thinks she's gonna find him too. Silly ole woman. Don't nobody want us."

Celeste glanced over at Willie T. They were both surprised at Mamma Bouvier's comment. Celeste responded quickly.

"What do you mean? You are still beautiful. Look at your skin? There's not a wrinkle to be found anywhere."

Mamma Bouvier didn't blink an eye. She acted as if she never even heard Celeste's compliment. She continued bitterly. "Lena is out there right now making a complete fool of herself, grinnin' at every man walkin'."

This didn't sound like the ailing little woman who had been standing on the platform asking the community for forgiveness. Celeste could tell that there was still some of the old 'Big Mamma' left in her frail little mother. But she said nothing. They continued walking arm in arm. And just as quickly as the old Big Mamma appeared, she disappeared. The gentle little 'Mamma Bouvier' was back, speaking softly.

"Celeste, I wish you would have at least written to Lena. She went through so much with me over you. She always loved you."

Celeste lowered her head in shame. "I know, but I just couldn't do it. I didn't want to deal with anybody down here..."

Mamma Bouvier interrupted. "...I understand. You wanted us all to go away, and I can't blame you."

Celeste stopped walking. "No, I never wanted you to go away. I loved you both. I just wanted to forget all the things that happened here, and I didn't know any other way to do it."

Mamma Bouvier began limping even more. "I'm just a little tired with all this excitement. Would you take me home?"

"I'll take you wherever you want to go. Willie T., would you like to ride with us? That is, unless your family is here, or you've got an appointment or something."

"No, I would love to ride with you. My family didn't come with me. They're still in Washington. And my parents are out here somewhere having a good time. I'll see them again tonight."

The wheels of the notorious BMW were off and running again. Mamma Bouvier's expression as the car peeled out of the parking lot was precious. She was horrified. Willie T. wasn't too happy from the back seat either.

"Celeste?" Mamma Bouvier asked.

"Yes, Mamma?"

"We ain't in no hurry."

"Oh, I'm sorry. Bad habit."

Celeste drove on more slowly - for a little while.

The BMW quickly passed by the riverbank, but nobody noticed that the ragged old man was still down there watching the water. Celeste wanted to ask about Bubba, but didn't know how to bring it up. "How is - everybody - down here, Willie T.?"

"Are you asking about Bubba?"

"Yes. I looked for him at the park, but I didn't see him..."

As soon as Mamma Bouvier heard the name 'Bubba', her chest rose as she swelled up with emotion.

"...Celeste, will you ever forgive me for what I did?"

"That was a long time ago, Mamma. We are trying to put the past behind us, remember?"

"But..."

"...And I forgive you. I forgave you a long time ago. I just

189

didn't know how you felt until I got that beautiful invitation. Why didn't you write to me?"

"I did, but I kept tearing the letters up. I was never too good at sayin' I'm sorry. You always meant more to me than anything in this world. I don't know why I wanted to do such a thing to you. Maybe I was jealous of your innocence and beauty. I don't know."

Tears swelled up in Mamma Bouvier's eyes again as Celeste held her hand - until Celeste took another one of the curbs in the narrow road, at which time Mamma Bouvier quickly let go of Celeste and held on tightly to the dashboard. She was cute sometimes. Celeste smiled, and with both hands on the wheel now, she made an extra effort to slow down and drive more responsibly.

"What kind of work do you do, Celeste?" Willie T. asked.

"I am a Professor of Black History."

"I'm impressed."

Mamma Bouvier approved too.

"You always were a smart girl."

There was a moment of silence. Every time Mamma Bouvier thought of the past she became filled with sorrow. "I'm so sorry, Celeste... I almost ruined your life."

Celeste was truly forgiving. "But you didn't."

"But..."

"But nothing. I'm here and that's all that's important at the moment. Besides, how long do you think it took for me to figure out that it was you who paid for that mysterious scholarship I received? My grades weren't exactly the best in my class, you know."

Mamma Bouvier said nothing. She just smiled.

Celeste got off the back road and was now on the highway to Mamma Bouvier's house and shifted back up to 5th gear, and started speeding again. She didn't notice a police car approaching with red lights flashing.

"What does Bubba do for a living, Willie T.?" Celeste asked.

Mamma Bouvier answered the question instead. "He's the best Sheriff we got in all of these parts."

Just then the police car turned on the siren for a brief moment of acknowledgment. Mamma Bouvier was a bit startled. Celeste looked in her rear view mirror and saw the car.

"It's okay, Mamma. I can handle this." Celeste said as she put on her turn signal and looked for a place to pull over.

"I knew we were goin' to get stopped," Mamma Bouvier said.

Willie T. tried to make it better. "There was a time you could have gotten us out of this no matter who it was, Mamma Bouvier."

The minute he said that, he realized that it was just not the thing to say. He felt really bad. "I'm sorry. I didn't mean..."

Celeste looked in the rear view mirror as much as she could without going off the road, and interrupted with..."Did you say Bubba is a Sheriff, Willie T?"

"Yeah."

"Is Bubba married?"

"Yes, but I haven't seen him in a few years. Last I heard, his wife was sick."

Mamma Bouvier updated them both. "She died last year. She was a nice girl."

Celeste found a place to pull over. "I'm sorry to hear that."

The police car parked a slight distance behind them to run a check on the license plate. Celeste's hopes had come true. It was Bubba. His hair was different, though. He had a nice neat haircut, and his face was clean-shaven, and his body looked to be in excellent condition. Celeste continued to focus on her rear view mirror. Willie T. watched her stare in the mirror. She looked at Willie T. through the mirror and winked. He figured it must be Bubba in the Sheriff's car. Bubba got out and proceeded cautiously. He looked even better out of the car. Celeste smiled with approval. He was bigger than Celeste remembered, and his shoulders were even broader than ever. His spotless well-pressed uniform left little for the imagination because it looked like somebody had cut it out and glued it to his Hulk Hogan physique.

Mamma Bouvier got restless. "What's takin' him so long?"

Celeste smiled seductively. "He's coming, Mamma. He's coming."

Willie T. decided to break the shock for Bubba. He jumped out of the back seat and went to greet him.

"Bubba! It's good see'n you, man." They hugged.

Celeste watched from her mirror. She waited patiently. It was obvious that Willie T. was telling Bubba who was in the car. Bubba's expression brought back good memories for Celeste. She wanted to just jump out and grab him, but she was a lady now, so she waited. He came to the door. Celeste got out.

"Hey, Bubba," she said seductively.

He was speechless at first and then... "Hey, ah - Hi - ah Celeste, you look good."

The sparks rekindled. They were in love all over again.

"You look good, too." Celeste could just die from excitement. Mamma Bouvier lowered her window and spoke dryly through the opening, but smiled pleasantly. "Hey, Bubba."

"Hey, Mamma Bouvier!"

Celeste was amazed at the respect those two seemed to have for each other.

"Celeste, Honey?" Mamma Bouvier motioned for her to come to the car window.

"Yes?" Celeste asked.

Mamma Bouvier's voice was much softer and lacked expression, but her sense of humor still existed.

"Bubba and me are good friends now, so you don't have to stand out here on the side of the road." Mamma Bouvier invited them all to her home.

* * * * *

Everybody was sitting around having coffee. There was no alcohol to be found. Celeste was amazed. She and Bubba sat on the couch. Mamma Bouvier sat across from them, and Willie T. relaxed at the nearby table. Celeste didn't quite know what to say to Bubba, but she tried. "I hear you lost your wife. I'm so sorry."

Bubba didn't really like to think about it, but Celeste was so sweet and sincere that he knew he must respond. "Thank you."

"How many children do you have?"

"Two."

"Do they live with you?"

"No. What about you?"

Celeste hesitated before answering. "Me? I never married."

For a brief moment Celeste thought back over her last forty years. What she wasn't about to tell them was that she had spent more time in therapy than out. She didn't want them to know that every time she found a good man she ran him away with her suspicions and paranoia, and an uncontrollable desire to recapture the passion she had had with her first love, Bubba.

Willie T. saw that this conversation was about to become a downer so he decided to pick it up a bit. "Bubba's daughter is attending Spelman College in Atlanta."

"That's where I went to school!" Celeste was pleasantly surprised.

"Yeah?"

"Yeah."

Bubba was truly amazed at Celeste. Not only had she maintained her beauty, even though she had to be in her fifties now, but she had done something that a lot of people could not. She had completed her education and gone on to a very impressive career. "She is really some woman," he thought to himself as he smiled and listened lovingly to her rattle on about Spelman. He watched her mouth as she laughed and talked about the sororities and professors who taught things that Bubba had never heard of. But after a few moments his smile disappeared. He began to think about what might have happened if she had not gone away. Aside from a possible battle between himself and Celeste's mother, he thought about what might have happened if she had stayed with him. He tried to imagine her barefoot and pregnant, or lying ill in their county hospital, waiting to die of something that the doctors couldn't get medicine for - like his precious wife.

"Where is the other one?" Celeste asked, but Bubba didn't answer. His face had broken out in a cold sweat, and he seemed to be off in another world. Celeste didn't know what was wrong with him. "Bubba, are you okay?" She asked.

"Oh, yeah. I'm fine. What did you say?"

"I asked you where your other child is."

"John Edward Jr. is married. He lives over in the next county. He would have come, but he had to work." Bubba reached in his pocket and got his handkerchief and wiped his face. "Man, it's hot today."

Bubba looked so good to Celeste that she could barely listen to anything he said. It had been a long time since she had had her hands on a good man. All she could think about was getting him alone somewhere. "So, do you live alone?"

"Yeah, would you like to come over before you leave?"

Celeste knew that she wanted to jump up right that minute, but she played it cool, and with genuine respect. "That's sweet of you, but only if you are comfortable with it."

"I think I can handle it." Bubba blushed.

Well, Willie T. got the two of them past first base. He was always good at resolving other people's problems. That's why he became a preacher. He always said that his 'calling' was to help others.

Willie T. remembered when he got his first church. It seemed that everybody in the congregation had issues that needed resolving, and so Rev. Willie T. Hightower thought he had died and gone to heaven. The men respected his ability to solve the most complicated problems with the simplest answers. And the women loved him for his ability to get the husbands to see their side of issues that only a woman would usually understand. Willie T. was the next thing to being a Saint in the eyes of North Eastern Washington DC and he loved it.

"Bubba, when is the last time you had a vacation?" Willie T. asked.

"Well, I..." Bubba couldn't remember.

"You know, every man needs a vacation now and then."

Mamma Bouvier decided to join in on the conversation. "I still got a little influence around here, John Edward. Your vacation can start whenever you want it to."

"Thank you, Mamma B."

Bubba tucked his head and sipped his coffee. Celeste smiled realizing that he was still shy after all these years. That was one of the things she had loved so much about him. She knew that she was hooked all over again as she slowly ran her index finger around the brim of the delicate gold rimmed coffee cup.

"You're welcome, John Edward," Mamma Bouvier replied.

Willie T. chuckled, "I still have a hard time saying John Edward. It still sounds funny to me." They all laughed.

Bubba admitted, "Even my boss calls me Bubba."

Celeste thought to herself, "I don't care what you call me,

just call me! And tonight wouldn't be too soon." She was hot for Bubba.

Willie T. asked, "Is Sheriff Tiddle still around?"

"No, he's long been dead. His wife killed him for messin' around." Nobody noticed that Mamma Bouvier didn't laugh along with the others. They just continued reminiscing.

Bubba remembered something he had wanted to ask Willie T. for years. "Willie T., now that we are grown adults, will you please tell me somethin' I been wantin' to know for a long time?"

"What's that?"

"What was it you use to put on your fishin' hooks to catch all those fish when we were kids?" Before Willie T. could answer, Bubba began to tell the ladies about how clean Willie T. used to be, and how he wouldn't touch a worm or get his shoes dirty.

Willie T. laughed, "It seemed like it was just yesterday when we use to do that stuff. Do you know I haven't been fishing since then? I don't even remember what I used to use. Most of the time it was just something from my mother's icebox. I never would tell you because half the time I was too embarrassed at what was really in that pail. I think meat loaf was the one I used the most. My mother cooked more meat loaf than McDonald's got hamburgers. And when I didn't have meat loaf, I probably used bread." They all laughed.

Celeste realized that somebody was missing. "Whatever happened to Walter Lee?"

Bubba looked at Willie T. Mamma Bouvier immediately got up to leave the room. She didn't like to talk about the past, especially Walter Lee or Sheriff Tiddle because she was the reason Sheriff Tiddle's wife killed him. And the guilt of what she had done with all those young boys was too much for her to deal with.

"I hope ya'll will excuse me. I'm feelin' a little tired."

Celeste recognized that Mamma Bouvier was uneasy, but she didn't realize what it was about.

"You want me to come and help you, Mamma?"

"No, I'll do fine. Ya'll make yourselves comfortable."

They all watched as she went slowly to her room. Willie T. was sad for a moment. "Time sure goes by fast, huh?"

Bubba watched the door as it quietly closed behind her.

"Yeah, seems like yesterday we were playin' out in the fields and shootin' baskets in Walter Lee's home-made hoop."

Celeste asked again. "Where is Walter Lee?"

Bubba didn't enjoy talking about Walter Lee, but he finally responded. "Probably down by the river. He stays there most of the time, except when he needs liquor. He'll come to town for that, and then head right on back out to the woods and that river."

Celeste didn't understand. "The river?"

Bubba explained. "Yeah, ever since Cleotus drowned, Walter Lee ain't been right. And the older he got the worse he got. It was when his Uncle Pete died that he totally lost it."

Willie T. gave Celeste a brief history on Walter Lee.

"Walter Lee and I are cousins. His mother and my mother were sisters. His parents were killed in a car accident when he was ten years old, and he always felt it was his fault because Uncle Nat and Aunt Mary were coming to get him from our grandma's house when they were hit by a drunken driver."

Celeste reached for Bubba's hand as Willie T. continued his story.

Meanwhile, in the bedroom Mamma Bouvier leaned her cane up against the wall and braced herself as she sat on the nearby vanity chair to take off her shoes and support hose. She was exhausted, excited, and sad, all at the same time.

The exhaustion was caused by the obvious. The reunion was a big success. Mamma Bouvier had worked on it for more than a year with her once young accountant, Xavier. Yes, he finally forgave her, too. The Howard University graduate never did leave Louisiana. That reunion in the late fifties was so suc-cessful that he was offered a partnership in one of the biggest accounting firms in the state. He also helped a lot of local peo-ple learn how to handle their money and property.

And now the reunion was over, and all Mamma Bouvier wanted to do was sleep. Her excitement, of course, was the return of Celeste. It seemed unreal to have her daughter come back to her with such pure beauty, love and forgiveness. Yes, this was truly exciting for Mamma Bouvier.

But finally, there was her sadness. Nothing could be sadder than to have so many negative memories brought up. Memories that Mamma Bouvier thought she had buried forever. Memories that hurt so deep in her heart she couldn't even afford to listen to her guests talk about a single one of them. Her soul ached with sadness.

Willie T. had moved to Mamma Bouvier's big chair. Bubba's arm rested gently on the back of the sofa behind Celeste. They sat close together, listening to Willie T. tell about his life with Walter Lee.

"My mother and father said that Walter Lee blamed himself because he was supposed to come home that morning with his grandfather who was coming this way, but instead, he decided that he wanted to stay a little longer, so his parents had to come and get him. Walter Lee was standing right across the road from the accident, and saw it happen. This did something to his mind. It really bothered him growing up, made him have a lot of disciplinary problems. My parents were going to raise him, but he chose to stay with his daddy's best friend, Uncle Pete. He said he felt more comfortable there. Less disciplined, he meant. He knew that my parents would make him go to church and he hated church after this happened. But I still tried to look after him."

"Uncle Pete died two years ago and the bank took the house," Bubba said.

Willie T. was upset. "I didn't know he had no place to stay! Nobody told me. Do my parents know?"

"Yeah, they know, but they can't do anythin' with him. I think they're kinda' scared of him."

Willie T. still couldn't understand why nobody had told him.

Bubba explained the best way he could. "Willie T., your life in Washington has been one of the greatest things that happened to this place. Everybody is proud of you, but - you've - always been - focused on - impressin' people, and - tryin' - to be..."

Bubba didn't know how to tell Willie T. that he was a snob, and that nobody really wanted to be bothered with him and his citified ways. But Willie T. already knew what Bubba was getting at. He had heard it before. He knew that this was difficult for Bubba to say to him because of their brotherly love, so he finished the sentence for Bubba. "...Uppity? Is that what you're tryin' to say?"

Bubba nodded 'yes.' And that was okay with Willie T. He knew that at times during his growing years he had been a little off-putting, but he also knew that if he had not focused on his dreams and ambitions, that he would be stuck in these backwoods forever, and he didn't want that. He knew that people didn't understand him, but he also knew that he had to do what he had to do. Now, he's got to figure out a way to explain this to his old best friend. So, he moved his chair away from the table and got as close to Bubba as he could, and looked him in the eye.

"Bubba," he said, "At no time in my life have I ever felt too good for my family or friends. It's just always been my belief that God put me on this earth for a purpose, and I wasn't ever going to make Him disappointed in me."

Bubba and Celeste listened quietly.

"I have never been one to compete with others, or try to keep up with somebody else's good fortune, and be 'Uppity.' I have just been trying to do what I believe is God's will, which is to help my people have a better life. And I know I can do more for my people in Washington than if I stayed here." Willie T. waited a moment for a comment from Bubba, but he didn't get one, so he continued. "And in order to be accepted in the big city, there were things I had to readjust in my life, but I never forgot who I am, and where I came from. Do you understand what I'm saying?" Willie T. wanted so much for his old buddy to understand him and respect his decisions.

"I understand. But, there are so many people needin' so much down here..."

"I know that, but I can't do for them down here. I can only do for them by getting laws changed up there, in Washington - by letting the government know how our people are ailing. And they won't listen to somebody from down here. They only listen to what they think are their own kind. And I have finally won a little of their listening power, and I can do more if I'm just given the chance. And that chance is right around the corner. I can feel it, Bubba. I am going to run for a political office, and I think I have a good chance at getting it."

Celeste understood what Willie T. was saying and tried to make Bubba understand better. "Bubba, if we had more Willie T.'s in the government, our brothers and sisters, like Walter Lee, would have more places to go to get help. He's just trying to do his work his way. You're doing the same thing here, being a good sheriff. It's just harder to understand when somebody is so far away. Willie T. is still accomplishing the same kind of work as you are."

Bubba replied, "I understand."

Willie T. was relieved to hear that. He reached for a hug from Bubba. "I'm really proud of where I came from, man. Nobody can change that, ever."

Bubba hugged him back. "I love ya, man."

Celeste poured more coffee. They all seemed to feel better now. However, Celeste was still not finished with the Walter Lee situation. "So, what do we do to help Walter Lee?"

"Sometimes I get him to come home with me and take a bath and eat something, but he goes right back out to the river where he can drink in peace," Bubba replied.

Celeste came up with an idea. "Maybe we ought to go and get him, and try to help him."

Bubba felt he had tried everything he could think of to help him."What will we do with him?"

Celeste felt that it was time for the 'woman' to take over. "Is this the Louisiana Family Reunion, or what?"

Willie T. tried to think of ways to help. "I could get him into an alcoholic treatment program."

Bubba responded quickly. "He needs more than an alcohol program."

Celeste was determined to make something work. "I could get him on an assistance program that would give him psychiatric help."

The two men thought quietly. Celeste wanted an answer. "Well?"

Chapter 14

Walter Lee sat on the river's edge staring at the rushing waters. A large log floated down the river. Walter Lee spotted it. Once again he became very alert. He sat up straight so that he could see the log better. For a brief moment Walter Lee was like the 16-year-old boy his friends remembered. His eyes were bright, his energy was high, and he was suddenly cute again with his mannerisms.

"There he is!" Walter Lee watched the log come closer. "I knew it! He's comin' back again! He's giving me another chance! I'm gonna make sure to save him this time!"

For all those years Walter Lee had been waiting at the river for Cleotus to come back. All this time he had been living the incident over and over, trying to find a way to kill this pain that was eating him up inside. It was like he had been placed in a Twilight Zone and couldn't escape. And the alcohol didn't seem to help either, so saving Cleotus was his last chance. And he thought if he could save his good buddy for sure this time, with no mistakes, things would be all right.

"I'm coming, Clee! Hold on! I'm coming!"

Walter Lee quickly removed his old coat and hat, and then his shirt. "I'm gonna get you this time!" He yelled breathlessly. "You hear me, Cleotus? I got you covered!"

He dove into the water with the rest of his clothes on.

Back on the road the BMW was off and running. Celeste seemed quite comfortable speeding down the back roads, but Willie T. and Bubba weren't. Bubba was sitting in the front seat with his seat belt almost up around his neck.

"Damn, it's somethin' else when you got the Sheriff scared." Bubba remarked.

Celeste smiled. "Just relax. I'm not going to hurt myself."

Willie T. was finally getting used to her driving even though he still held on for his dear life. "I think I'm fallin' in love with this car."

Celeste smiled again. "Rides nice, doesn't it?"

Willie T. agreed. "Yeah. I like the way it takes the curves.

"You do?" Bubba was not seeing things the same as Willie T.

The beemer pulled on to the road by the river. Bubba pointed to the spot. "Right over there."

They parked and got out and started down over the embankment. It was a little muddy, but nobody seemed to mind. They were determined to find Walter Lee. Bubba called out for him. "Walter Lee? Walter Lee, you down here?"

They looked around. Finally, Celeste spotted him out on the rocks. She grabbed Bubba's arm and pointed. Walter Lee looked like he was holding on to something and smiling.

Willie T. didn't understand what Walter Lee was looking at. "What's he doing?"

Bubba tried to figure it out. "I don't know." Bubba called to him. "Walter Lee?"

Willie T. stepped in. "Let me try it. Walter Lee, it's me, T-Bone!"

Willie T. got up on a higher part of the embankment so that Walter Lee could see him, but it didn't quite turn out that way. Walter Lee heard them calling him, but his glassy eyes showed nothing but confusion. He looked over at the three people, smiling. He was soaking wet, and that big object that he was holding turned out to be a log.

When Walter Lee finally focused on Willie T., he thought that he was looking at his dead Uncle Pete. Willie T. called to him again. "Walter Lee, it's me!"

Walter Lee really believed that he was seeing his Uncle Pete. "Unc? Uncle, is that you?"

Willie T. continued to try and get through to him. But all that Walter Lee could see and hear was his uncle…

"Walter Lee, come on over here. You're gonna fall in that river!"

Willie T. didn't realize that Walter Lee had already been in the river numerous times over the past 40 years; saving Cleotus over and over and over again.

From the embankment Willie T. talked to Celeste & Bubba. He was anxious to help. "We've got to do something! He can't stay out on that rock!"

Willie T.'s heart was sinking at the sight of this pitifully lost soul holding on to some inanimate object as if the entire world depended on his not letting go.

Bubba was upset too. "He thinks you're his Uncle Pete. Sometimes he has hallucinations. I think it might be the wine."

Celeste stared at Walter Lee. "He definitely needs help, but I don't think it's the wine."

Willie T. couldn't take this. Tears swelled up in his eyes. He didn't like seeing Walter Lee in this condition. "Why hasn't anybody called me?"

Bubba could barely speak. "I've never seen him this bad."

Willie T. was determined to get Walter Lee off that rock. His heart was filled with compassion. "Walter Lee, it's me! T-Bone! Come on over here!"

Walter Lee yelled from the rocks. "I've got Cleotus! I got 'im! I caught Cleotus! And he's okay! I got him right here! And I ain't lettin' him go this time! I can't let him go, Uncle Pete!"

Willie T. spoke to him through Uncle Pete. "We know you tried to save Cleotus, Walter Lee. Everybody tried."

Walter Lee stood his ground. "But I didn't try hard enough!"

From the riverbank, Willie T. cried. "We all tried, Walter Lee. We all tried. God knows we tried."

Walter Lee continued to argue with his Uncle Pete. "You wasn't there, Unc! You wasn't even there! I was there, and I didn't go to him. I didn't go when he asked me to. I didn't go when he was slippin'. I could'a made it there in time if I had come when he asked."

By now Walter Lee began to see not one person on the embankment, but three. This really confused his already bewildered mind. "Who is that with you, Unc?" Walter Lee squinted his eyes causing the last drops of river water to slide quickly down his cheeks and drop on to his heaving chest. "Who is that?"

Celeste and Bubba didn't know what to say as they looked at each other with concern. Celeste encouraged Bubba to do something. "Well, who are we? If you tell him who we really are, he might get even more confused. Tell him something, Bubba."

Well, Bubba was just about as dumbfounded as Celeste. "I don't know what to say."

This was probably the first time in Willie T.'s life that he couldn't talk his friends out of a situation. He was so perplexed by the entire situation it left him speechless.

Finally, Walter Lee solved the problem himself. "Mommy? Daddy? Is that you?" Walter Lee was smiling from ear to ear. He could not believe his eyes. What a perfect time to visit, and just when he had done the most heroic deed of his life. "It is! You came all the way out here to see me do the right thing." Celeste and Bubba were numb with fear of saying the wrong thing.

Willie T. was numb, period. They must have stood silent for only a few seconds, but it seemed like a lifetime.

Willie T. began to come alive by doing the one thing he believed in most, prayer. "Dear Heavenly Father, we stand here in these woods today praising Your name and thanking You for all your many blessings, but at the same time, Lord God, we are severely lost in a moment of anguish and hopelessness."

Celeste grabbed Bubba's hand as they bowed their heads and stood silently under the big willow tree where Walter Lee so often slept.

Willie T. continued, "God, we ask you to look down upon us at this time and give us the strength and understanding to assist Walter Lee, our brother."

Walter Lee sat on the rock silently holding his log. It was almost as if he knew that Willie T. was asking for the Lord's help.

"Please help us, Lord God, to lead him out of this lost and troubled life. All this we ask in Your precious name, Amen."

At that very moment, it appeared that God had truly listened. Walter Lee lowered the log, and stood up and looked over at his friends. And even though he was still confused and upset, something was happening to him. He wasn't crying anymore. A part of him knew that Uncle Pete and his parents were dead, but the sick and needy part thought that his precious loved ones, who had long passed on, were truly standing on the riverbank talking to him.

Celeste began to encourage Willie T. to do something. Anything! "He thinks you're his uncle, Willie T., so talk to him like his Uncle Pete would have!"

Willie T. was so disheartened. "Yeah, yeah, I know. I'm thinkin'. But Walter Lee thinks that the two of you are his mom and dad. What's wrong with your mouths?" For once Willie T. was trying to pass responsibility to someone else. And he made a good point. But Celeste couldn't answer him, and Bubba just stared across the water at Walter Lee with a completely blank expression. So, Willie T. knew that once again it was going to be up to him to resolve a bad situation. So he decided to pretend to be Uncle Pete. "I - love -ya, Walter boy. I love you." But this turned out to be more difficult than Willie T. had anticipated as he began to cry again, "We - love - you."

All three friends started to cry uncontrollably, and before they knew it they were all suddenly speaking as if the very spirits of Walter Lee's family had come to assist them.

Bubba found words, "Walter Lee, we're all here for you."

Celeste confirmed, "Yes, Walter Lee, we're here - to help you, and we do love you so much. And we'll never leave you."

Celeste looked over at Bubba. She was feeling something that she had never felt before, not even in church. She was consumed with emotion for someone she hardly knew. But Bubba couldn't help her. He was too filled with the spirit himself. He just knew that his love for Walter Lee was bigger than life, and that something or someone was directing him to save Walter Lee, no matter what the cost. Willie T.'s prayers were truly being carried out. The air was thick with blessings, and they all could feel an unexplainable excitement.

Walter Lee looked so pitifully lost out on that big rock, the very same rock that he had stood on 40 years earlier when

Cleotus cried for help.

Willie T. continued to speak on behalf of Uncle Pete and pleaded with Walter Lee to put the log down and come back across the water. "You didn't do anything wrong, Walter Lee. Cleotus is at peace."

For a moment it appeared that Walter Lee was finally figuring things out. He seemed to be really battling with the reality of who these three people were. It was obvious that he was trying, but he just couldn't get his thoughts in order.

Walter Lee listened to his uncle and his parents a moment longer as they continued to yell, "We love you." And then slowly he raised himself up and looked toward the sky. Still holding on to one end of the log, he broke out in full cry... "Oh, God in Heaven! Please take me to my mamma! I need my mamma so bad! I just want her to hold me. Can't somebody - hold - me, please? I've needed holdin' for so long."

From the riverbank, Bubba made a very serious decision. He didn't care what the other two would say. "I'm goin' after him."

As Bubba took off his gun, shirt, shoes and belt, Willie T. decided to do the same. "Not without me!"

Celeste was filled with deep emotions, as the men were about to make a major attempt to cross the raging river and embrace their troubled friend. Willie T. took off his expensive suit, but hesitated before he removed his pants. He looked at Celeste. She just smiled as if to say 'do what you gotta do.' Willie T. hung his suit on a tree branch and dove in behind Bubba. They both swam hard, fighting the rough current. But, as Celeste suspected, the rushing waters made no difference to

Bubba or Willie T. The men were truly filled with the Holy Spirit, and no raging waters or unfamiliar floating objects were going to stop them from getting to the other side of the river to be with their brother-in-love.

Both men made it across with little or no problems. Soaking wet and tired, they joined Walter Lee on the rock. From the embankment, Celeste could see the two men trying to take the log from Walter Lee and talking to him, but Walter Lee wouldn't let go of it. They struggled with him, as Celeste watched with concern.

Finally, Willie T. tossed the log into the water while Bubba held Walter Lee, who was struggling and crying. Willie T. went over to the two men and held on to both of them. Willie T. and Bubba hugged Walter Lee with all their might and then rocked him like a baby as he cried in their arms.

* * * * *

Willie T. went back to Washington DC, but not before he and Celeste set up a complete program for Walter Lee. They convinced him to commit himself to a very good institution for the mentally disturbed. They saw to it that he was given such a good healing program, that he would probably be out and able to resume a life for himself in just a few years. Bubba had promised to visit him often, and to keep the other two informed of his progress. Bubba also promised that he would do everything in his power to help Walter Lee find a home of his own when he got out.

Celeste and Bubba spent the next two weeks together. However, they made sure to include Mamma Bouvier as much as possible. The ailing woman may have been old and sickly, but this reunion made her happier than she had ever been in her life. She had never remembered enjoying her very own family before. She and Celeste had never been able to show such love for one another, but they could now. Mamma Bouvier's prayers had truly been answered.

Finally, the time had come for Celeste to leave Louisiana. As Bubba put her luggage in her car, it was obvious that he didn't want her to go nor did she want to leave, but she had to get back to work.

They kissed passionately. "I've had a wonderful time, Bubba. My two-week vacation turned into three weeks, and I couldn't be happier. It's been a good three weeks."

Bubba smiled and agreed as he held her close to him. He didn't want her to go. He said, "This was like the first time we were together, only this time I fed you." They both laughed.

Celeste leaned into him as he rested against the side of the car. "Everything was delicious... and so were you." She hugged him. They kissed. "You know, I can't believe I was so dumb at sixteen."

"I think naive is a better word. Sixteen in those days wasn't what it is today." Bubba continuously rubbed Celeste's face and arms. He loved touching her, and he knew that it might be a long time before he would get this chance again.

"I think dumb is dumb," Celeste pouted.

Bubba stared at Celeste's mouth as she spoke. He loved this well-spoken, well-groomed and citified woman. "You weren't dumb. I think you just closed your eyes to what was goin' on around you."

Celeste appreciated his comforting words, but the truth was the truth. "I was dumb." They both laughed.

Bubba was so full of love for her he didn't know what to do, but he did know what he couldn't do, and that was to make her stay with him. There was nothing in this county that she could want, and nothing outside this country town that he could cope with. So... "I wish you didn't have to go, but I understand."

"I'll come back again."

"I hope so. Just don't try to make it another forty years, or neither one of us will be around." He smiled. She hugged him. "I won't. I promise."

Bubba opened the door for her. She got in the car and rolled the tinted window down to talk. "Check on Mamma sometime, will you? She seemed tired this morning."

"Don't worry. I'll go by there first thing tomorrow."

"I love you." Celeste said as she reached through the window for one last kiss.

"I love you too." Bubba made it short and sweet.

They stared at each other as she slowly rolled her dark window up. And before they could blink twice, the shinny black turbo was once-again flying down the back road to New Mexico. Back to the city life.

* * * * *

Lena drove up to Mamma Bouvier's house in high spirits. She

grabbed her things out of the car and raced up to the house and entered without knocking. "Emma? It's me, Lena!" She put her jacket and purse down and looked in the mirror to check her nylons. Her little legs almost filled out her stockings, but she didn't notice the baggy calves because she was so excited and talking fast. And even though Lena was in her seventies, she still managed to tip around gracefully in high heel shoes, and she looked pretty good doing it. She had really grown old gracefully, despite the fast life she had led.

"Girl, that man I met at the reunion was somethin' else! His name is Jamal. That's a different kinda name, huh?" She looked around for Emma as she continued talking. "He ain't left me alone since. I like him so much. He's somethin' called a Muslim. Can you imagine that? Me, with a man of God? I'm old, but I guess I still have it." Lena giggled like a little girl on her first date as she continued to search for Emma. "That's why I ain't been around much." Lena kept expecting Emma to show up, but she didn't. "Emma, you ain't mad at me are you?" Lena went to the kitchen. Emma wasn't there. She called for her again. "Emma, where are you? I think we're gettin' married!" Lena looked out in the back yard and then went down the hall to Emma's bedroom.

The late afternoon sun had moved to the other side of the house causing Emma's bedroom to be somewhat dark. However, there was just enough light to see Emma lying quietly in the center of her massive king-sized bed. Lena tried to focus her old eyes in the semi darkness. "Emma, you in here?"

Mamma Bouvier appeared to be reading something. As Lena got closer, she could see that Emma was holding the Holy

Bible that was opened to Psalms, Chapter 51. Lena knew something was wrong. "Em...?" She touched Emma lightly.

At that moment Emma looked slowly up at Lena and gave her an unusually slight smile, and said weakly, "I promised God I would take care of her, but - I didn't do - a very good job, huh? Mamma did though." Shortly thereafter, she closed her eyes for the last time.

Lena stared at the still body for a long while wondering why her best friend had said that. But, once Lena realized that Emma was gone, she didn't think about anything else accept her ace boon-coon, Emma Celestine Bouvier, was dead. Lena then lost all control of herself. She began to cry and touch Emma on her hands and face and hair.

"Emma? - Emma Bouvier, you wake up now, you hear me?" Lena tried to wake Emma up by gently shaking her, but it didn't work. Lena was so full of emotion she could barely speak.

"Oh, Lord. Oh, Jesus Oh, my Emma. My best friend - Oh, please -don't leave me. I can't make it - out here without - you." Her body went limp as she fell to her knees beside the bed. But, after a while a real calm came over Lena. She started talking to Emma as if she were still alive.

"Em, my new man is - a nice man. He don't know nothin' about us. He don't know what we did, and he don't know who we were. He thinks I'm somethin' special, Em. He'll respect you too. If you would just wake up." Lena cried quietly.

"Please don't go-o-o, Em. We done found our forgiveness. God sent him to us."

After long hard tears, she stopped and paused. "I love you, Em."

Lena climbed in the bed with Mamma Bouvier, crying quietly. She got as close to her as she could, and just lay there and looked at the Bible, and held on to her best friend, Emma Celestine Bouvier.

At the same moment as Mamma Bouvier's death, Celeste was on her way back along the highway to New Mexico when suddenly a warm feeling filled her body with unexplainable emotion. It was almost as if a soft warm wind had passed right through her entire body. Celeste almost wrecked the car. When she finally got herself together, she pulled over on the side of the highway. The sound of the gravel underneath the BMW's tires drowned out the sound of the woman inside the car screaming in agony over her mother's death. Yes, somehow Celeste had sensed that her Mamma Bouvier was gone.

The scripture that lay open in the Bible read:

> *"Have mercy upon me, O God*
> *According to thy loving kindness:*
> *According unto the multitude of thy*
> *Tender mercies blot out my transgressions.*
>
> *Wash me thoroughly from mine inequity,*
> *And cleanse me from my sin.*
>
> *For I acknowledge my transgression*
> *And my sin is ever before me."*
>
> *Psalm 51: 1-3*

THE END

ABOUT THE AUTHOR

Audrey Lewis is one of the few women to join the elite circle of independent filmmakers. She wrote, directed and produced a film entitled "THE GIFTED". This blend of fictional and real characters won her an induction in the Black Filmmakers Hall of Fame in 1994 for her screenplay and picture. In 1997 she produced another feature film, "A MOMENT OF ROMANCE", for Hong Kong China. (She is one of few, if any, females to produce an anamorphic film).

Audrey's career in the arts began in fashion design at the Art Institute of Pittsburgh and extended through a stint as a fashion model, modeling director, teacher and actor. Having produced numerous stage works, she was employed in various production positions at most of Hollywood's major studios.

Her ability to meld facts with fiction carries over in this latest adventure - a tale of victimization and sexual abuse - of typical growing pains of youth and untypical consequences exemplifying the masks of comedy and tragedy.